THE SPIDER:
SATAN'S DEATH BLAST

THE SPIDER

MASTER OF MEN!

SATAN'S DEATH BLAST

By Grant Stockbridge

ALTUS PRESS • 2019

CHAPTER 1
THE SPIDER FALLS

A N EAR pressed to the door, Richard Wentworth heard muffled voices, then the scrape of chairs thrust back. His lips tightened beneath the skirted black mask that hid his face. He whirled down the hall.

"Upstairs," one of the conspirators had mumbled. "It's safer there."

Safer from spying eyes and prying ears, they meant. They would leave a man downstairs to guard against surprise. They did not know the Spider was already within their lines....

Wentworth reached ancient stairs in a bound, went up them three at a time. Only the faint creak of the old risers betrayed his spurring feet, and that sound was swallowed up in the careless, heavier tread below.

The voices below rumbled on, became sharply distinct—the door had been opened—and Wentworth flung up the final steps, caught the banister post at the head and hand-pivoted around it. A window at the front of the hall was covered by a cracked shade. Threads of dusty sunlight pierced it and revealed a door on each side of the hall. Wentworth chose the left, eased it open. The room was empty. He ducked in as the conspirators' feet mounted.

Within the room, wooden chairs made a circle around a cigarette-scarred table. Two windows, with broken shades drawn,

let in trickles of light, and across the room from them was another door. Wentworth raced to it on quick, light feet, fingered the knob and peeped through the slit. Darkness beyond. It was a closet.

The footsteps were in the hall now. Would they go into the other room or enter here? Either way, Wentworth was ready. He could listen in the hall or from this closet…. The knob turned, the door pushed inward. Instantly, Wentworth was out of sight, shut in the closet. His hand slid to the automatic holstered beneath his arm and he waited tensely. The chances were against these men investigating the closet, but he had

2

Bloomington, Buffalo and Albany were devastated by the Devil's blasts.

heard enough already to know that discovery meant death. He knew that these men had some vast plot under way, a plot that meant millions to them and death to thousands. What it was he did not know, but....

"What's that door over there?" The voice, rasping and irritable, seemed to vibrate within Wentworth's skull. The man meant the door to the closet in which he was hiding! He heard footsteps slap toward him and eased his muscles for swift action, slipped the automatic clear.

"Don't be a fool, Hines," another voice cut in. It was whining but nasty. "Don't be a fool. It's a closet."

"There, there, my children!" There was gentle mockery in this new voice, mockery—and something else that was flat and evil. "Always quarreling. Be nice, boys, or—*there will be discipline!*" Those last words were like a whiplash.

WENTWORTH HEARD chairs dragged up to the table and he pressed close against the door to listen. The man of the mocking voice, obviously the leader, was speaking again.

"If you boys have decided to be good," he jeered, "I'll tell you the immediate plans. In minutes now, the opposition will be crushed. When Beach *goes up in dust,* they will give us the park lands without any further trouble. No one, not even Beach, has the slightest idea why we want those lands."

"God! *Up in dust!*" The whine was a whisper of dread.

Wentworth, crouched in the closet, heard the words with tight anger. He knew the man they meant. It was Senator Calles Beach, his friend, and the man whose philippics against the Park Bill had brought Wentworth to Albany. The bill provided that all state parks be turned over to a private corporation represented by Delancey Howard, a lawyer. They made various promises about preserving them for public use and improving them.

Of course, the measure had caused a furor, but it had been Senator Beach who had chiefly fought the thing. He suspected fraud, and Wentworth had decided to look into the matter. He had come to Albany only this morning and watched the office of the corporation lawyer, Delancey Howard. From there, he had followed a man here.

What he had found was ten thousand times worse than fraud. They planned to murder Senator Beach! And what was the hellish instrument of destruction that they planned to use? *Up in dust*, the leader had said, and even his own henchman had seemed awe-struck. It must be horrible indeed if the conspirators who used the thing feared it also. But the leader was speaking again….

"When Beach's destruction proves our strength, the others will come to heel like whipped curs," he went on softly, mockingly. "Within two weeks of the time the land is ours—within two weeks, we will be too powerful for the Government of the United States itself to overcome!"

Wentworth frowned, shook his head sharply.

What power could the mere possession of several thousand acres of park land give these men? What fearful plans did they have that they deemed themselves able to defy even the mighty government at Washington?

How long would it be before they tried to murder Senator

Beach, Wentworth wondered. He had always admired Beach as one completely honest legislator. The senator played no politics and he always defended the people. He had seen in this bill only the theft of the lands from the public. But what Wentworth  had heard proved the steal was only a small part of the plot. Here was murder and huge menace against the government!

Beach's earnest doughty face rose before Wentworth, his mane of white bristling hair, his prize-fighter build. Death must be creeping upon him, stalking its prey in some unimaginably ugly form while Wentworth waited in this closet, listening to his assassins talk.

If he burst out of this closet now, shooting, he might save his friend. He could kill these conspirators. But would that block the plot?

"Four minutes now, and Beach goes up in dust!"

The man's laughter was more mocking than his speech. "Let us observe four minutes of silence for our dear friend, the senator. Then when we have received the sad message of his demise, we can go our ways sorrowing."

"To hell with that!" Words rasped out impatiently, "If we keep quiet four minutes, every time we kill somebody, we won't ever talk."

Whining laughter. "That's right. You can't loot cities without killing a few!"

A few? Good God, it would be thousands! They were planning to sack cities, spread ruin and murder and rapine....

"Are you through talking!" The leader was speaking again, the words like a whiplash, the tone fearful. "I think I'd better silence you two now before your foolish chatter causes any serious trouble." The deep voice was soft and gentle—and horrible! "Did it ever occur to you that you talk too much?"

WENTWORTH, LISTENING, stirred with a growing, nervous impatience. Talking, talking! These men were calmly talking, and in four minutes his friend, Senator Beach, was to die. The gun in his hand had an inviting weight. He could thrust open the door and shoot three times swiftly, dash for the stairs. Albany was not large. It was scarcely three blocks from here to Beach's home.

"We'll keep quiet, Isong! Honest, we'll keep quiet!"

There came the flat smack of a blow.

"I said you talked too much!" The voice was deadly cold now. "Do you want to go *up in dust?*"

The words drew a yelp of absolute terror. All of the conversation was being recorded indelibly in Wentworth's sensitive mind, though he heard it but dimly because of the struggle within himself. Should he save Beach—or learn more of these plotter's plans? Beach was a defender of the people even as was Wentworth, save that Beach had chosen the channel of legislation and Wentworth had become the Spider.

Wentworth was an independently wealthy man, the sole living member of a rich family. Probably he would have become one of the nation's greatest authorities on criminal law, except that during college his intimate friend and counselor, Professor Brownlee, had fallen into trouble through the machinations of a rival who coveted his position and his wife. That man had framed the old professor and there had been no escape for him, save through that man's death. To save Brownlee, Wentworth had killed the man cold-bloodedly and on the dead man's forehead had traced in blood the figure of a hairy-legged spider.

Thus had the Spider been born. Wentworth had turned more deeply to the study of the law and had found that, on every side of him, the law served more to protect than to snare the criminal. He saw men whose records of murder were known on every hand freed in the courts because their dominion was so strong, their strength—and wealth—so great that juries and prosecutors and witnesses feared to operate properly. He saw innocent men suffer, saw the guilty prosper. And many of these could not be touched within the law!

So Wentworth had dedicated his life to the righting of wrong, to the battle with the octopus Underworld which yearly extended its tentacles more and more deeply into the vitals of the nation. It was to the Spider alone that countless thousands owed the preservation of their lives and fortunes from criminals, thousands who did not even know his name—except that now and then in the newspapers they read that the notorious criminal called the Spider had killed another man and printed his red, menacing seal upon his forehead.

Many times Wentworth had risked life and fortune in titanic battle. Many times in his crusades of justice, he had been forced to choose between friendship or love and the furtherance of his fight against crime. And now it was posed for him again, Beach's life or his larger duty to society—which could be served only through the destruction of this evil which, unsuspected, threatened the lives of many. But already he had heard enough, hadn't he? Murder. Looting of cities! A death that transformed a man to dust! A gang that within two weeks could defy the entire power of the nation!

A thin smile twisted Wentworth's mouth. He turned the knob slowly, kicked the door open and bounced out into the room with his automatic in his hand. Two men had their backs turned. A third faced him, and for a mad moment, Wentworth thought it was the Devil himself who crouched across the table. Satanic evil sat upon his features. Black points of mustache and imperial sharpened a bony, ridged face. The eyes were narrow and slanted upward, and the thin lips leered.

For an instant the tableau held while Wentworth's piercing gray eyes glinted through the slits of his mask into that face out of hell, then the two other men whirled. Their chairs crashed to the floor. Their guns flipped out.

WENTWORTH SPRANG toward them and the men reeled backward to clear their guns. It gave the Spider the instant he needed. His automatic spat twice. One man staggered, tripped over his chair, and falling with a clatter, did not move. The other merely collapsed.

The Devil-faced man was raising a gun slowly.

He held a scarlet cape before him like a shield so that only the evil leer of his eyes showed above it. Wentworth dropped beneath the table. His gun blasted upward and he saw the red cape jerk and quiver with his lead. The Devil fell.

From the hall came the pounding of feet. The door slammed wide and a crouched giant of a man came in behind a raised revolver. A bullet pushed him against the wall, but his gun hand stayed up. His lead spewed into the room, thudded on the table. The thunder of his shots was deafening. The hollow walls beat it back and magnified it a hundred times.

Wentworth fired again, and the gunman seemed to shrink, with his elbows crushed against his stomach, his face twisted in pain. He bent forward at the waist slowly, pitched on his face.

Wentworth kept his eyes on the red-cloaked figure of Devil-face while he went swiftly over the pockets of each body—while he pressed the base of his cigarette lighter to the brow of each man who had fallen before the Spider's swift lead.

Then Wentworth crossed to Devil-face and, gun poised, drew the red cloak slowly aside.

The man's shirt was crusted with crimson. The sharp, ridged face seemed still to leer up at him. Wentworth felt with a thin shiver up his spine that the Devil-faced one was still alive, as if he were some Mephistopheles who could rise beside his own pierced body and, laughing, live to kill his slayer.

He half raised his automatic, then shook his head sharply. The Spider did not mutilate his kill. Warily he leaned forward and pressed the base of his cigarette lighter to that ridged forehead. And when he had taken his hand away, a small red spot flowed like blood on that demoniac face, a spot of red that was like an evil blood-shot eye, except that there were hairy legs upon it. Wentworth smiled grimly as he gazed upon his calling card of death—*the seal of the Spider!*

But there was no time to delay here. Three of the four minutes Beach had been allotted for life must have passed. Though he had moved swiftly, it had been necessary to search these dead for possible clues to others in the plot. Once police had come, it would be too late.

And already a whistle was shrilling in the street outside! It was probable that at least two patrolmen on nearby beats would answer on the run.

Wentworth sprang through the door, jerked it shut behind him and went down the stairs in a rush. In the back hall, a phone was fastened to the wall. Luckily, he knew Senator Beach's number....

"The Senator there? Ann? Listen, Ann, this is Dick Wentworth. Men are plotting to kill your father this minute.... Yes. Find him fast and tell him to get behind cover, to let no one approach him.... Yes. I know he goes for a walk every day at this time. What? He's on his way to the State House? Then hurry, for God's sake, hurry!"

He slammed up the receiver, streaked down the back hall. He must hasten, too. The death intended for Beach might strike the governor, too.

CRA-ASH!

The hall filled with the reverberations of a shot.

White hot pain stabbed through Wentworth's thigh. His leg gave way and he went down, rolling to cover behind the stairs.

11

His jaw clamped shut beneath the mask. He had been shot through the thigh, wounded in the first encounter with the conspirators!

There was no feeling in his leg, and it refused to hold his weight. But he must escape. He had slain four men and printed his seal upon their foreheads, the gun that had slain them was in his pocket and police were closing in. Even as he struggled to rise, glass smashed in the hall and Wentworth knew a policeman had broken the front door panel to get in.

Wentworth gouged torturing fingers into his wounded thigh to strengthen the muscles, fought to his feet with a hand braced against the wall. He staggered into a room to his right, heard the door whang open behind and police feet pound in the hall. He put his hand to the window to throw it up, then cursed between his teeth.

In the back yard, pounding toward the house, was another policeman, gun in hand. The Spider was trapped by police, and the Spider did not war against the forces of the law! Even as Wentworth limped back from the window, the policeman outside spotted his moving shadow, his masked face, and threw up his pistol!

CHAPTER 2
BEACH GOES UP IN DUST

THE POLICEMAN'S lead dug into the wall by Wentworth's head with a sullen thud, and a round hole with radiating cracks fractured the window glass. The Spider dug his fingers more deeply into his wounded thigh, and made his heavy crouching way to a door beneath the stairs.

He was listening intently. The slapping feet of the policeman who had crashed the front door were silent now. That shot had thrown a scare into the cop, given Wentworth a second of grace.

One second. Wentworth had made good on less margin than that. He eased through the door into the dark coolness of the basement. Sweat beaded his face beneath the close black mask. He shut the door without sound, caught the banister with his free hand, and vaulted himself to the cellar floor with a single leap. He bit his lip violently to choke back a cry of pain. Two more wound-tearing hops on his one good leg, and he had reached the outer cellar stairs.

They led upward beneath two wide wooden covers that slanted out from the house and formed a trap door. Tense beneath them, Wentworth heard cautious feet above. The cop was creeping up on the cellar doors to a window. The Spider's clenched white lips twisted in a slight smile. For a brief moment he leaned weakly against the stone wall, then, fighting faintness that was like a weight upon his chest, battling intolerable pain, he eased up the outer cellar steps until he crouched with his shoulders against the wood, his good leg braced solidly.

His gun was in his pocket now. What good was a gun against police? Though the Spider might violate laws, he did it only because those laws themselves had been twisted until they protected the very criminals they were supposed to curb.

Braced against the trap doors, he tensed his body to act—and light flooded the cellar.

Wentworth twisted his head and saw blue trouser legs on the top step. The second policeman was descending into the cellar. Wentworth waited no longer. Rallying every atom of his strength, he heaved upward on the trap doors.

A man yelled in fright. The doors banged open and Wentworth, hauling himself out of darkness into sunlight with a single mighty heave of his arms, spotted a policeman sprawled upon the earth. The man's gun was ten feet away and he was tangled with empty ash cans. Wentworth made two long springs on his one good leg, the shock of each biting like the torture irons of the Inquisition into his wound.

He reached the fence that hedged in the narrow yard on the right, snatched up a clothes pole. He straightened, half blind with the sweat of pain. The policeman struggled clear of the ash cans, dived for his gun. The window of the house flung upward.

Wentworth held the pole across his body, one hand at its end, and took four great striding leaps across the yard. Guns banged. Lead sang a deadly song past his head. A bullet jarred the wood in his hand. The Spider thrust the end of the clothes pole in the earth, threw himself upward and sailed clear of the fence.

He made the garage door and heard bullets whang into the iron side. There was a car within. Wentworth pulled himself along its side to the front door. Keys in the lock! He used the palm of his hand on the starter, thrust the car into reverse and sent it caroming backward into the yard—but Wentworth did not go with it. Instead, he flung through a small window in the side of the garage and into the street beyond.

NEW GUNFIRE burst out behind. He picked up a barrel stave to use as a cane, and bracing his wounded leg with it, stripped off the mask and hobbled along the street. He heard a rending crash as the car wrecked itself, more shooting. A man in a window saw him, but flinched from the threat of his gun and fled. He would describe the man he saw fleeing with his trouser leg drenched in blood; but he would describe a man with a heavy black mustache, who carried his head a little to one side, a man with shaggy black hair on his neck—and the Spider did not mind these things, for these were only part of his disguise, not the real Richard Wentworth.

He reached the corner. A car with a woman in it was waiting for a green light. Her eyes were fixed on the traffic standard. Wentworth took two long hops forward and her face twisted about, startled beneath a jaunty red hat.

"I'm a police officer in disguise," he said hurriedly. "There's a murder going to be committed near the State House." He opened the back door and heaved in. "Get me there fast!"

The woman turned completely around in her seat, staring at Wentworth with her eyes wide open and her lips shut tightly.

"Hurry!" Wentworth bit out. "Don't wait on traffic lights." He leaned forward, showed a key glinting in the palm of his hand. "There's my badge. Now get going."

The girl jerked the car forward, grated into second and whined around a corner before she hit third. Wentworth threw a quick look about him. Narrow Main Street with its lumbering street

15

cars and congested traffic was a half block ahead. The girl slapped her hand on the horn and held it there. People on the sidewalks turned startled faces. A truck blundered deliberately into their path.

The girl wrenched, skated past its nose with a grating of fenders, whirled into Main Street and spurted up the left side of a street car, dodged back in front of it with a clear street for a block ahead. She jammed the gas all the way down, took time to flash a wink at Wentworth in the rear vision mirror. Her golden hair was streaming in the wind. Wentworth nodded, lips tight. She could drive.

A cop sprang into the middle of the street and Wentworth leaned from the side window yelling and waving his key in simulation of a badge.

"Bandits!" he yelled. "Their car's ahead!"

The policeman jumped aside as the car bore down on him. He was uncertain and left his gun hanging at his side. Wentworth settled back in the rear seat, took out a handkerchief and bound it tightly over his wound. He could at least stop the blood. He took a nearly emptied clip from his gun, slid a fresh charge into the butt.

Four minutes, Devil-face had said, and Beach died. Four minutes! It had been ten since he had pronounced doom upon the senator. Was Beach dead or had Ann, thanks to Wentworth's warning, reached him in time? What new and terrible weapon did these criminals propose to use?

The girl slid the Ford in front of a taxi, spurted into broad

State Street and charged up the steep grade toward where, behind the park, the State Capitol spread its imposing mass.

Wentworth tensed forward on the seat, his wounded leg stiffly braced against the violent leaping of the Ford over the cobbles. The Park! There was Senator Beach! As far as he could see him, Wentworth would know that short-legged, belligerent stride, that hair bushing out from beneath an inadequate hat.

The Spider flung a swift glance behind him, to left and right about the park. A few men sat on benches: a woman strolled with a dog on a short leash. That was all except—yes, there was Ann Beach, too, running bare-headed from a side street toward the park. Perhaps even yet they were in time!

SENATOR BEACH checked his striding, struck a match, moved it toward a cigar with cupped hands. The Ford was a block away now, motor roaring. Wentworth clenched his automatic, kept his eyes searching for threat of attack.

"Slow!" he called to the girl behind the wheel. "Slow!"

A hurricane of hot air struck him in the face. His breath was driven back into his nostrils. He felt the car stagger, sweep back and sideways with a crashing of glass and a ripping rasp of torn metal. Intolerable white glare blinded him and he went deaf. He felt a pounding as of immense weights upon his brain, then a vast numbness.

When that receded bit by bit, Wentworth began to move his hands erratically. He twisted his head, braced away from the cushions and realized he could see. The girl who had driven him was limp in the front seat, her head lolling back and her golden hair torn as if by a gale. Her little red hat was gone, and blood dripped slowly from her nostrils.

Wentworth reached out a wavering hand and touched her throat. The pulse was there, a little uncertain, but healthy enough. He stared about him. Their Ford was jammed against a building, its side driven in.

The Park was devastated. Trees were snapped off and stripped of foliage. The benches were a litter of wreckage, and the men who had loitered there…. Wentworth's grim eyes flinched from what had been human beings, sought out the spot where Senator Beach had stood. There was a crater there as if a high explosive shell had burrowed and convulsed the earth.

From the way in which the wreckage was strewn, it was apparent that had been the center of the explosion, but of Senator Beach there was no slightest trace. Not even a blood stain on the pavement.

Senator Beach had *gone up in dust!*

Shaking and weak from loss of blood and the effects of the terrific blast, Wentworth thrust himself out of the battered car, drew his automatic and moved toward the spot of the disaster. His ears popped, and not until then did he realize he had been deaf. When he heard the sounds that came from every side, he wished that he still were deaf. The suffering screams of the wounded filled the air. The body of the woman who had held the dog was smashed against a tree. He knew it was the same woman because the dog's leash was embedded in her flesh.

The portico of the Capitol had crumbled, and every window on the square was a gaping black hole. Autos had been crushed against buildings as if by battering rams. Only the fact that the Ford in which Wentworth had ridden had been in the middle of a broad street that permitted the force of the blast to be dissipated had saved them. Senator Beach had lighted a cigar charged with explosive, and this had happened!

Suddenly Wentworth understood. That was why the murder had been late. Usually Beach lighted up the instant he left the house. It was a habit of his that he followed as regularly as his meals, as regularly as the walk he took at a set time every day. But today, he had violated that rule and only a few moments of time had prevented his cigar from blowing the Capitol with him up in dust!

Wentworth leaned heavily against the shattered trunk of a tree. Devil-face was dead, but his machinations went on after him. Their few words of the plot had indicated a vast body of criminals bent on murder and pillage. And great God, what a fearful weapon they had! An explosive which in the minute quantity a cigar could contain, was powerful enough to wreck a building nearly a block away, to kill a half dozen people within a radius of yards! Powerful enough to blow to dust, to disintegrate a human being!

In two weeks, Devil-face had said, not even the government could put them down. The government? Good lord, not all the world could suppress such power! But Devil-face was dead. Perhaps....

Wentworth looked slowly about him. A black limousine purred from a side street across the southern side of the square. Instinctively Wentworth hurled himself prone, rolled and crouched in the crater where Beach had died. A machine gun chattered into the bright light of the day; lead burned the pavement.

Cautiously, the Spider raised his head when the racket stilled, peered along the pavement, and saw, framed in the window of the limousine, the Devil-face of the conspirator!

For a terrible moment, Wentworth wondered if the man was indeed a fiend who could not be killed. The chill edge of horror that had knifed up his back as he stood over the man's body came back and paralyzed him. He saw the ridged, evil face twist into a mocking smile, saw the snout of the machine gun thrust from the window again.

CHAPTER 3
THE DEVIL STRIKES

WITH A violent wrench of will, Wentworth broke the spell that seemed to bind him. He hurled himself backward and down, as once more the hot spatter of lead, the evil cackle of the machine-gun filled the sunlit day. Once more and it was gone.

Wentworth rolled and watched the broken edge of the torn pavement. If the Devil should dash to the crater to pour down a single burst, the Spider's only chance would be a swift and unerring shot.... He waited, eyes alert on that pavement, jagged against the tender blue sky. Minutes dragged past, then slowly he dragged himself upward with hands braced against the slanting sides of his prison. He had heard the long-delayed wail of police sirens, for once a reassuring sound to the Spider.

He peered over the brink of the crater. The black limousine was gone. Laboriously, he pulled himself out of the hole and, once more with his barrel stave cane, made his way slowly across the square. Ambulances were jamming hub to hub into broad State Street, into the narrow way that bordered the park. White-coated men were running with stretchers. Two darted toward him, an intern racing with them.

Wentworth shook his head.

"There's no great hemorrhage," he said, "and I can walk. Take some of those who can't." His grin was hard. He did not want a doctor to discover a bullet wound to connect him with that other man with a wounded leg who had pole-vaulted from a house where the Spider had killed four men. Wentworth narrowed his eyes as he struggled haltingly on across the park. Four men? The Devil had been one of those and he had not been killed!

Wentworth tried to recall whether the red glimmer of his seal had been on the forehead of the man with the machine gun. That seal was a tattoo that could not be removed short of gouging the flesh on which it was printed. Slowly Wentworth's finely chiseled lips lifted into a brittle smile, his gray eyes grew hard as onyx. Never before had a living man worn the seal of the Spider, but it doomed him as certainly as if the Black Widow's dread poison burned in his veins.

Wentworth limped on, his eyes bitter as he surveyed the damage of the blast, the dead and the dying. He saw Ann Beach revived and started for home in a taxi, saw the blonde girl who could drive like a demon being treated at an ambulance and sent off to a hospital with a broken arm…. He would get her name there. A check might help compensate for her injuries and her smashed car….

Hobbling away from the square, he was, despite his injury, an impressive figure of a man, shoulders broad and athletic, tapered slim hips that bespoke power and endurance, an arrogantly poised head. His face, its grim outlines clear beneath the battered remnants of his disguise, was strong and commanding. It was the face of one born to rule, one who could dare greatly for an ideal—or die for it if necessary.

Such was the man who had become the Spider to save the country from the pillaging hordes of the criminal world. To most, he was Richard Wentworth, wealthy clubman, sportsman and amateur criminologist extraordinary, dilettante of the arts. To a few he was the Spider, nemesis of all crooks, the mysterious avenger who spread terror—and with it law-abidance for a time—wherever his dread red seal of death marked his kills in the name of justice.

ON HE hobbled, in his blood-crusted, shabby clothes. At the corner of Hartshorne and Dagly, where homes secluded their porches behind lines of hedges and thick-grown shade trees, he whistled thrice shrilly and with a peculiar lilt. A moment later the sleek snout of a luxurious Lancia slid out of an alley and purred up beside him.

A Hindu, his turban gleaming white against a dark and anxious brow, sprang down and flung wide the door. He assist-

Ram Singh, the faithful, struck straight and swiftly, at Wentworth.

ed Wentworth into the rich tonneau, and fury glinted in his dark eyes. His lips were tight against fine white teeth. For when a man harmed Richard Wentworth, he stabbed his servant, Ram Singh, to the heart.

"My rooms, Ram Singh," Wentworth ordered.

He sank back wearily into the velvet cushions, feeling faint now that the need for maintained vigilance had for a moment relaxed. Ram Singh hesitated a moment, but at Wentworth's slight gesture, he sprang to the driver's seat and wheeled the Lancia along back streets and by round-about ways to the Hotel Laurelton. He sprang down and opened the door, and Wentworth, his disguise removed, his shabby, blood-stained clothing replaced by fresh garments from the secret wardrobe of the Lancia, stepped slowly from the car.

"Garage the car, Ram Singh," he dropped over his shoulder. "Return swiftly."

Pain ran searing fingers up and down his leg.

The dressing was a mere absorbent pad taped on to last until he could reach his room. He paused at the desk, leaning an elbow on it to ease the strain on his leg. The clerk behind it was young and his cheekbones were shiny from the razor.

"Yes-*sir!* Mr. Wentworth!" He slid the keys along the desk. "A gentleman phoned, Mr. Wentworth, just a few minutes ago. Said he'd call again."

Wentworth eyed the clerk speculatively. He had many friends in Albany, of course, but he had notified no one of his presence except Senator Beach. And Senator Beach was horribly dead.

"No name, eh?" he said carelessly. "What kind of a voice did the man have?"

The boy leaned toward him, bright eyes blue and slightly protruding. He dropped his voice. "Deep, sir. He sounded like it was some joke. You know, laughing. I didn't like it, sir." He straightened, flushing. "I guess maybe I oughtn't to say that, but, but—"

Wentworth nodded, smiling slightly. "That was perfectly all right. Thank you." He slid a bill across the counter.

"Thank *you*, sir!"

Wentworth moved with his guarded limp to the elevators and went up five floors. When the boy slammed open the door, he waited a full thirty seconds before he went out with his hand upon a gun in his pocket. No one was in sight. Slowly he moved up the dim hall with its dark green carpet.

There was no doubt in his mind that the man who had called was the one he had dubbed the Devil. There might be an ambush in his room now, but Wentworth doubted it. There had been too little time since the machine-gun attack had failed and the call had been made. No, the chances were that the attack was yet to come…. When it arrived, Wentworth and Ram Singh would be ready.

He reached his quarters, used the key from the protection of the wall and thrust the door open, snapping his hand to cover also. No gun explosion blasted out; no poison gas hissed its warning. Wentworth entered hurriedly and made a swift tour of his rooms, pausing tensely to listen in each. But if there was a clock bomb in the rooms, he could hear no slightest, muffled tick of the machinery and well he knew the sound. He bolted the door and stripped to his underwear, baring corded hard thighs and tanned shoulders whose muscles slid like silk beneath his skin.

Slowly he untaped the temporary pad on his thigh and inspected the wound as casually as if it had been on some other person. The bullet had struck high in the left thigh from behind and lanced entirely through, just missing bone and femoral artery. Death had been as close as that for the Spider!

And now, handicapped by a weak leg, he faced warfare against a Devil man and a weapon surely conceived in hell! If they used it as they intended, hundreds, thousands, would die. Towns would be laid to waste, with millions of dollars' damage. Banks and stores would be looted. If they used it—and no power on earth could stop them, no authorities even suspected them—except the Spider.

WENTWORTH'S LIPS went thin with pressure. Slowly he extracted one of his privately blended cigarettes from its platinum and black case and tapped it thoughtfully on a thumb nail. He stared impatiently at the outer door. What the devil was keeping Ram Singh? He moved his tongue dryly. Feverish. The wound was throbbing and his thigh felt four times normal size.

He looked at the door again, gray eyes sharp, forced himself to lean back and rest in the stiffly upholstered chair while he waited. The cigarette was consumed, another lighted. He was frowning now, his eyes fixed unwaveringly on the entrance. He started when finally there came a light scratching on the panels.

Wentworth dropped his left hand into the cavity beside the chair cushion, closing his fingers around his automatic.

"Come in," he said clearly.

The door swung inward slowly. Ram Singh strode in.

"Lock the door," Wentworth ordered. His lids half concealed his eyes. Smoke dribbled up from his lips and he watched the Hindu through a veil of hazy blue.

"I am sorry for that I was delayed, *sahib.*" Ram Singh bowed. "A car bumped fenders and the man was quite angry."

Wentworth waved his cigarette impatiently.

"Hot water, Ram Singh, a basin of it, cloths, iodine and bandages. The bullet went all the way through."

Ram Singh bowed again, cupped palm to his forehead and crossed the room with his lithe, alert tread. Wentworth's head swung with him, watching. There was a curiously tipsy smile on the Spider's mouth. He drove it from his lips, sat up stiffly in the chair. He must not let the fever get him.

When Ram Singh strode back, Wentworth ordered the phone in a harshly unnatural voice. The Hindu remained impassive. He brought the instrument and plugged it into the wall and Wentworth called New York, the apartment of Nita van Sloan. Her voice was lilting in his ear, richly contralto. The tension went out of Wentworth's body as he heard it. He sank back in the chair while Ram Singh went methodically about cleansing the wound.

"The call again, darling," Wentworth told her, and curiously there was a smile on his lips. There was happiness in the smile, but there was bitterness too. There were two great things in his life, the crusades of the Spider and Nita van Sloan, the one woman in the world whom he trusted with full knowledge of his work, the one woman in the world who claimed his unwavering devotion and love. That was what brought happiness to his lips now.

But even before their love, came the labors of the Spider. Not until he had wiped crime from the earth, or until there was another to carry on the task where he dropped it could their love be consummated in marriage. It was an oath he had sworn; it was the pledge between Nita and himself. So when he smiled there was bitterness there, too.

Nita's voice over the wire was calm, but he felt the tightening of her white throat upon the words. "The thing you expected, Dick?"

"That and much more, *cherie,*" he told her. "I need you here, my beautiful. Come and bring Jackson in the Northrup, tell Professor Brownlee to read the papers and believe all he reads about the explosion in the park here. Tell him all that explosive was contained in an ordinary cigar. When I can I'll send him a portion of it to analyze."

He thrust aside business now, talked of other things as he pictured Nita's lovely self before him, Nita with her clustering curls of chestnut, her glorious eyes of blue beneath her so black brows that were like silk, her red curving lips.

He half-closed his eyes, talking. He let go the automatic and held the phone before his lips with both hands. His eyes jerked wide. Without warning, Ram Singh had sprung toward him!

As he leaped, his hand jerked clear the razor-edged knife that always lay hidden in his belt.

Ram Singh, the faithful, Ram Singh, his slave to the death, drew back the footlong blade and struck swift and surely at Wentworth's throat!

CHAPTER 4
RAM SINGH, THE FAITHFUL

W ENTWORTH SAW death in the eyes of the faithful servant. There was fury there, fury and hate and venom. The knife blade flicked forward unswervingly, driven by Ram Singh's powerful hand. There was no time for a word, no time even for thought. What happened next could never have been accomplished by a lesser man than the Spider. Only his split-second trained reflexes saved him.

He thrust the French phone forward to meet the knife, used it like a foil to turn the blade. It slithered by his throat so close its razor edge burned the flesh. Like lightning, Ram Singh struck again.

As the blade darted forward now, Wentworth struck with the phone. Not upward at the head. He could barely have reached that, slouched down as he was in the chair, and his blow would not have been half strong enough to hurl Ram Singh aside. He struck at the arm, aiming shrewdly at the nerve center just above the elbow where triceps and biceps muscles merge.

The blow had the double force of Ram Singh's thrust and

Wentworth's powerful wrist, and the knife flew from the Hindu's paralyzed fingers. It caromed from the arm of the chair to the floor with a thin musical tinkle. Wentworth could hear Nita's excited voice vibrating over the wire. His lips shut in a grim, straight line.

Lunging forward, he caught Ram Singh's fierce charge on his shoulder. It slammed him back in the chair and a gouging hand reached for his throat. He was pinned against the stiff upholstery, fingers like steel talons biting into his throat.

The phone, jammed between them, was hurting Wentworth's chest. He dropped his left hand down beside the cushion and grasped his automatic. A shot would end the battle. Wentworth jerked the pistol up, but he did not fire. He slammed the flat of it hard behind Ram Singh's ear.

The Hindu's head jerked away from the blow, but his hold did not loosen. With the world whirling blackly before his eyes, Wentworth struck again and Ram Singh's fingers relaxed. He slumped and with a thrust Wentworth rolled him to the floor.

He drank in the air in great thankful gasps, caught the phone to his lips. "It's all right, Nita," he got out hoarsely. "Just a minute." He heard the eager, excited rush of her voice and leaned back against the chair, the heaving of his chest subsiding slowly. "It's all right, darling," he said again. "Someone attacked me, and I had a bit of trouble quieting him."

"Wasn't Ram Singh there?" came Nita's sharp query.

Wentworth smiled faintly, his eyes narrowed. "Yes," he said quietly, "but he got knocked out. Hurry and come, darling. I'll look for you this evening."

He broke the connection, heaved himself up stiffly and stood looking down at Ram Singh. Laboriously, he dropped on his good knee, the other leg rigidly held behind him. He forced up one of the Hindu's eyelids. The pupil was wide, his breathing deep and slow. Wentworth tilted up the man's chin and closely examined the throat, did the same with each arm. On the left biceps he found what he sought, the mark of a hypodermic needle.

Laboriously, then, he made his way to his bags, busied himself with vials and a hypodermic and returned to Ram Singh. He made an injection in the throat; then slowly massaged the back of the neck, pressing hard at the base of the skull just above the nape. Two minutes of that and Ram Singh moaned, tossed his left arm restlessly and his eyes flickered open. He stared without recognition up into Wentworth's face, then his eyes focused and bewilderment clouded his face. He tried to get up.

"Just lie quietly for a few moments, Ram Singh," said Wentworth soothingly. "Think now. What is the last thing you remember?"

RAM SINGH looked quickly into Wentworth's face, then closed his eyes and his face grew impassive. He lay like that for a full moment. "I remember, *sahib,* that a man's car crowded against yours and bent a fender. The man got out very angrily and said bitter things. He had an evil face like a demon's and he had the eyes of a hypnotizer. Then someone seized me from behind. That is all I remember, master."

He opened his eyes and looked up again at Wentworth, with a trustful worship that was like a small dog's. Wentworth nodded slowly and got to his feet with the help of the chair arm. He sank into the seat.

Ram Singh got alertly to his feet. "Has anything happened, *sahib?*"

Wentworth shook his head slowly. "Nothing, Ram Singh. That man used drugs and hypnotism on you. He probably questioned you about me, but if he had not already known my identity, he would not have seized you, so that there is nothing lost, no damage done. Of course, while you were under the influence of hypnotism, you were not responsible for anything you did. You were obeying the will of the Devil, not your own."

Ram Singh saw his knife, the overturned basin of water. His eyes opened and his face grew strained. He dropped on his knees, held the knife before him with the point toward his heart. He forgot English and poured out his native Hindustani.

"Oh, master, if I have offended thee, say but one word and this unworthy one will atone."

He tensed his arms to drive home the knife, its point pressed against his breast, his eyes fixed with that same dog-like worship on his master's face. Wentworth's eyes probed deeply into the soul of the man and found no wrong there. Well he knew that if he so much as frowned that blade would be plunged deep into Ram Singh's heart. He had no doubts of his servant's faithfulness. He had but fallen prey to the evil genius of the Devil whom his fellow plotters had called Isong. Here was a bitter foe, a man who fought with subtle weapons, a man who sought to kill through the hands of another…. Truly, here was a worthy opponent for the Spider, one that would call forth all his swift strength and strategy. Wentworth smiled slowly into the eyes of Ram Singh and shook his head slowly.

"Thou art my faithful one, O Ram Singh," he said quietly, speaking in Hindustani also. "Not even the planets in their swift flight about the sun are more true to their destined course, than thou to me. Thou hast done nothing to offend." He touched the hilt of Ram Singh's knife with the first two fingers of his right hand. "Thy blade is honorable, O Ram Singh!"

Ram Singh gazed fixedly into his eyes for a full minute and slowly peace spread over his face. He got to his feet and slid the knife back into his belt sheath. He bowed, touching cupped hands to his forehead in a low salaam. Pride was in his eyes.

"The *sahib* has made his servant whole again," he said.

Wentworth nodded gravely. He felt suddenly weary. The struggle had broken the coagulation of blood upon his wound and the bandage was red again. But there was no time for rest. The Devil would not rest. Even if he thought Wentworth disposed of through his hypnotism and drugging of Ram Singh, he would not rest. The Spider, to him, was simply an enemy destroyed, as he had wiped out Beach, so that he might push on with the looting of the nation's cities with this terrific explosive that could destroy a man like a puff of cigar smoke.

Wentworth drove himself to the labor of dressing, replacing beneath his left arm the compact tool kit that the Spider was never without, drawing on dark gray tweeds, settling jauntily into place a brown *Borsalino* felt—even in the dead heat of summer Wentworth preferred its light coolness to stiff straws or sportier panamas.

Then, with a cane for his left hand he managed to walk, without too obvious an effort, across the room.

He turned at the door. "I'll take a taxi, Ram Singh. Remain here and when the *missie sahib* arrives, have Jackson bring the car over to the home of Senator Beach. I will return within the hour."

He went slowly down the hall, his face a little pale beneath its healthy tan.

DOWNSTAIRS THE shiny-faced clerk was babbling about the explosion. "Twelve people killed, sir! Yes, *sir!*"

Wentworth's eyes grew hard at this proof of the Devil's power. He offered no comment, but made arrangements for Nita's quarters and went out with the clerk's cheery "Yes, *sir!*" echoing behind him.

A taxi did fancy traffic cuts with him through Main Street, turned north on Mac Henry past small frame and brick homes,

Richard Wentworth

wound through Grosvenor Park where the lake lay beaten and still beneath the assault of the June sun, and drew finally out onto Lakefront Avenue where the mansions were old and sat back from the street like comfortable dowagers.

The gaping foundations of one were being filled in and bungalows, bright with unpainted yellow wood, were going up close to the sidewalk and close together. The dowager mansions seemed to sniff.... Wentworth smiled at the conceit and as the taxi braked and bumped across the sidewalk up the semi-circle of the drive before Senator Beach's home, he sniffed, too. A man in white overalls was squatting by a battered bucket before the new bungalows, dipping shingles in creosote.

The taxi deposited Wentworth at the door, and he made his slow-footed way up the weathered steps to the deep porch, across it to the triple glass panels of the recessed door. A maid whose eyes were red and swollen, opened it and stepped aside heavily. Wentworth proffered his card, and Ann Beach came into the hall to meet him.

She held herself proudly, her honey blonde head erect, her blue eyes direct, a woman taller than the average, whose simple black dress emphasized the clear whiteness of her face and throat. She offered her hand firmly.

"Good of you to come, Dick," she said quietly. "I ran, but—" Wentworth nodded. "I was there," he said.

"Anyone here?"

Ann Beach nodded, and Wentworth delayed in the hall. "Ann," he said quietly, "I'm going to talk to you as I would your father's son. The greatest assuagement of grief is action. Your father's death calls for that." She nodded, her eyes unwavering on his. "I know that."

"He died because he fought the park bill," Wentworth went on swiftly, watching the portièred entrance to the parlor where there sounded the faint murmur of two subdued voices. "There is much more behind that bill than even he dreamed," he said. "Murder and robbery and wholesale looting. I know only a few of the details, but I was wondering if your father's papers would give us any clue."

Ann Beach said slowly, "I doubt it. I kept them in order myself—but as soon as these others have left I will go over the papers carefully. I appreciate, Dick—" Her voice broke and she bowed her head and closed her eyes for a second. Wentworth's hand went to her arm. "I appreciate what you did, Dick."

"What I did was a failure," he said harshly, "but some have already paid for that death. And the defeat of their plans will be the final vengeance, Ann."

THEY WENT in through the dark red portières with their dangling tassels and a man arose, meticulous in white flannels, blue coat and a shirt of white silk.... Wentworth bowed to the woman at Ann's clear-voiced introduction. "Miss Patrici, Dick. Angelica, Mr. Wentworth."

The woman so introduced held out a white-gloved hand and Wentworth bowed again, lifting it to his lips, his gray eyes upon her own languid black gaze. She was a person of night-like darkness, her hair blackly soft beneath a white-piped hat of blue straw whose deep, tilted brim shadowed her face so that she turned her head slightly to look up at him.

"*Signorina,*" Wentworth murmured. He turned to the man. "Mr. Pierce, Mr. Wentworth," said Ann.

The man clicked his heels. His hand grasping Wentworth's was strong and solid, and his smile was pleasant.

"I have heard of you, Mr. Wentworth," he said heartily.

Wentworth smiled. "I know that voice," he returned. "On the air, I think. You're *J. Osborne* Pierce, aren't you?"

Pierce laughed and shook his head sadly, "I can't escape my fate," he said. "I am."

The woman turned her head slowly. She appeared never to move except with languid disinterest. Her hands in her lap seemed heavy. "I really think, Osborne, I shall have to deny myself the pleasure of your company. I can't have everyone knowing I go about with a radio announcer."

"Not an announcer, my dear," Pierce protested, laughing. "A commentator, if you please. The columnist of the air!"

It was light chatter. It seemed out of place in this somber house of tragic death, but Ann's lips curved in a smile that seemed even to extend to her eyes. She was the sort, Wentworth knew, who would never permit a public acknowledgment of her grief.

Through the windows, the bright sunlight of the late afternoon was gay, but the deep porch shadowed the room, left it funereal and solemn. The man in the white overalls who had been dipping shingles across the street had evidently quit for the day. With his coat over his shoulder, his hat on the back of his head, he was moving slowly off up the street. It must be after four…. The Lancia poked its sleek nose about a corner, lounged into the drive with Jackson's square-set shoulders behind the wheel. Wentworth turned to Pierce and the dark woman.

"Won't you join me," he said seriously, "in urging Miss Beach to accept a guard here? I am uneasy about this business. I'm afraid that the threat extends to herself."

Pierce frowned, pursing his lips. "After what has happened," he nodded, "I don't think you can take too many precautions. She should be guarded by all means."

Wentworth saw puzzlement in Ann's steady blue eyes. "Really, Ann, I think it is indispensable," he said. He gestured toward the windows, showing now the polished, rakish body of the Lancia, with Jackson wooden-faced behind the wheel. It was a landau, and Jackson sat in the open driver's seat, a trapezoid of sunlight splashed across his deep chest.

"Jackson," said Wentworth, "served with me in France. He was a sergeant and one of the best. Let me leave him with you to watch over your safety."

ANN SHOOK her head slowly, saw Wentworth's insistence. She continued to look at him. "If you really think it's necessary," she consented.

Angelica Patrici got slowly to her feet, the heavy silk of her dress settling itself gracefully about the smooth lines of her hips.

"You two have business to discuss," she said in her soft, accentless voice. "Osborne and I will go."

Ann did not protest. Her manner was always simple and direct. "It was nice of you to come so soon, Angelica. Osborne, I'll see you in the galleries."

Pierce bowed with his clicking heels. "It is very brave of you to carry on."

Ann's face was completely serious. "My father died because he fought the parks bill," she said deliberately. "If my presence in the gallery can sway a few votes against it, I certainly shall not permit any personal consideration to keep me away."

39

The two visitors left, and Wentworth summoned Jackson into the dim old room. Wentworth's voice was crisp.

"Jackson, this is Senator Beach's daughter, Ann. The same peril her father faced threatens her. I want you to guard her."

Jackson's brown eyes swung from Wentworth to the girl. She met them directly. "It sounds silly to me," she said.

Jackson smiled quietly. He had the heavy jaws of some Gascon forebear, wide beneath his close-set ears. He was shorter than Wentworth, but his shoulders were wider and he had bulky, quick muscles. Not a mere chauffeur, this man. Between him and Wentworth was a man-to-man understanding that dated back to No Man's Land, to a dawn raid and a machine gun nest… they had saved each other's lives a half dozen times, that night.

"If the major says it's necessary, miss," said Jackson with his quick, easy voice, "you can count on it that it is."

Wentworth smiled with lips that would not lose their grimness. "It is, Sergeant. I'm counting on you. Ann, you'll not lose a minute on those papers?"

The girl shook her honey-colored head slowly.

Her eyes were troubled.

"I won't, Dick." Wentworth clasped her hand once quickly and made his way haltingly to the door.

He cried out sharply. "Jackson, to arms!"

With a swift movement, he carried the cane to his right hand, and the handle jerked loose from the wood. A slither of steel, and he thrust a sword like a flash of lightning into the hall. A man cried out in strangled pain.

"Jackson!" Wentworth called again. "Guard Ann! We're attacked!"

CHAPTER 5
A VAIN BATTLE

WENTWORTH WAS battling furiously in the half-light of the hall. He could not lunge fully. His bullet-pierced leg hindered him. But his sword-cane blade made a glittering barrier. A gun blasted and he flinched aside, thrust violently and a man sagged on his blade.

Behind him, he heard the stamping feet of combat, heard the spiteful crack of Jackson's Luger. Ann's voice was sharp, "Behind you, Jackson! *Oh!*"

Wentworth lunged at a man, half-seen in the darkness, throwing himself forward on his bent right leg, reaching out full length into the hall. His left leg collapsed, dragged, and he spilled to the floor, stabbing up as he went down. A curse—and a gun clattered to the floor. The man whirled and fled.

Painfully, Wentworth dragged himself up, a hand braced against the wall. He jerked aside the portières and lurched into the room. Jackson lay on his face, blood upon his head. The Devil stood over him, a revolver in his right hand, his left knotted about Ann's wrist. The girl was straining back, her face distorted with terror, her honey-gold hair streaming.

Wentworth hopped laboriously to the attack, sword ready. He thrust savagely. The Devil glimpsed the light flashing from the blade, turned his leering, evil face. Deliberately, he yanked the girl to him, threw a pinioning arm about her.

Wentworth was in mid-lunge when the girl's body was jerked between his blade and the Devil. It was too late to check. He loosed his grip on the hilt and it clattered to the floor. He flung himself down, and the lead from the man's belching gun whipped the portière behind him. Ann was fighting with the frenzy of frantic fear, screaming unintelligibly hoarse sounds. She struck at the demon face, twisted and sank her teeth in the man's gun wrist!

Wentworth rolled, grabbed for his own automatic. With a curse, the Devil dropped the gun, jerked his hand free and struck Ann with a clenched fist. She sagged, as Wentworth pulled his own weapon and held it ready. He could not fire wildly, could not trust to a snap shot to drop this man who used Ann's body as a shield. Swiftly, the man backed toward the front windows. A creak of feet on ancient boards behind Wentworth forced him to jerk his head that way.

Two men sprang into the room behind him. His flash bullet caught the first between the eyes. His gun banged wildly. A window crashed in tinkling fragments. The second man threw himself prone behind the body of the other, eased his gun into view. Wentworth put a bullet through the hand and twisted toward the windows.

The Devil was out and pelting across the front lawn with Ann in his arms. Resting his arm on the sill, Wentworth fired three times deliberately. He saw the flying red cape jerk with his lead, saw the Devil stumble. But the man plunged on.

Wentworth's breath was harsh in his throat. The pain in his leg was like white hot steel. He dragged himself over the sill to the porch, fell and heaved up again. The jump from the porch was fierce agony. He flung a glance at the instrument board of his own car, cursed and staggered on, hopping like a wounded bird, dragging that tortured and worse than useless leg behind him. Jackson had the Lancia's keys!

THE DEVIL had reached a black limousine. As the Spider struggled on, the Devil thrust his unconscious prisoner into the back seat, flung himself in after her and clapped shut the door. Its sound was heavy and dull, the reverberation of armor plate. The chauffeur at the wheel meshed gears, and the car leaped forward, racing directly toward Wentworth. His gun was useless against it. Windows and body would shed bullets. A punctured tire would spell injury and possibly death for Ann Beach as well as for those criminals who were kidnaping her. He saw a window opened a narrow slit, saw the evil snout of a machine gun!

He flung himself toward a stack of shingles on the walk as lead spattered the pavement. The bucket of creosote where the overalled man had worked stood beside him. With a choked cry, Wentworth snatched it up. Bracing his left hand against the pile of shingles, he whirled the bucket high toward the street, just as the blunt, brute hood of the Devil's car thrust into view.

Wentworth flung himself flat, saw the bucket strike the top of the limousine and deluge it with creosote, saw it race on and heard the drum of bullets churn the earth about him, felt the stinging bite of clods rain in his face. But the car was going away fast, creosote dripping behind it. The backward-flung lead was poorly aimed.

It was a full minute before Wentworth was able to drag himself slowly erect and, balancing on his one good leg, look about him.

Frightened faces were white at the windows of nearby houses. A police siren was thin with distance. Down the street a blue-uniformed figure was running heavily. A gun glinted in one hand. In his other he clenched a night-stick. The law had come—too late!

Wentworth found a sawed-off length of board and putting it beneath his left arm as a crutch made his way laboriously back toward the Beach mansion. He could feel the warm flow of blood down his leg from the wound. It was sticky in his shoe. Once more faintness swarmed upon him, but resolutely, jaw clenched doggedly, he fought toward the house.

The pounding of the policeman's feet was audible behind him now, but he did not turn his head, only hitched himself stubbornly on toward the mansion. He had to get Jackson and pursue the Devil. He laughed a little wildly. Pursue the Devil!

The policeman's feet made softer noise, on the grass now, and he puffed up beside Wentworth.

"What's… what's going… on here!" he got out in gasps.

Wentworth laughed again, his voice shrill. "The Devil kidnaped Ann Beach," he cried. Then the board crutch slipped. He fell forward on his face—and blackness that would not be driven back swarmed in upon him.

CHAPTER 6
ARRESTED FOR KIDNAPING

WHEN WENTWORTH fought back to conscious-ness, his trousers had been ripped and a white-coated young intern was putting on the last wrapping of a bandage.

"If you don't keep off that leg," he said cheerfully, "you stand a damned good chance of losing it."

Wentworth nodded and thrust his heavy body up from the ambulance floor.

"Jackson?" he demanded. "Who's he?"

"Guy in the house with the broken head, chauffeur's uniform."

The intern thrust his head out the back of the ambulance and yelled: "Jackson!" There was a mumble of voices and the white-coated back retreated inward, turned and revealed a dapper little man with a crisp gray mustache just stepping up into the ambulance. He looked down at Wentworth with sharp, small eyes.

"Where's Miss Beach?" he demanded. Wentworth looked past him at the tooth-revealing smile of the intern. "This," said the intern, "is our chief of police. Name's Reed."

"Where's Miss Beach?" Reed repeated and his voice was sharp.

Wentworth let himself slowly back on the blanket, closed his eyes. "She was kidnaped," he said. "I'm Richard Wentworth. The man in the khaki uniform is my chauffeur, Jackson. We were in the house and some men broke in. We accounted for several, but one of them knocked out Miss Beach and ran out of the house with her. I followed, but he got away in a car."

"And these men you accounted for," Chief Reed's voice was dry. "Where are they?"

Wentworth opened his eyes and looked steadily up into the face of the wiry little chief. He had a ruddy face, and his sharp bright eyes were black. "The battle was in the hall and parlor," he said.

"The bodies, or the trail, if they were only wounded, should be there."

Reed stared down at him fixedly. "I've heard of you, Wentworth," he said slowly. "You have a way of dabbling in affairs that come to the attention of the police. Commissioner Kirkpatrick has vouched for you on occasion when you wanted information from us."

"All of which leads up to what?" Wentworth asked curtly. He had never had direct contact with this man before, but through Stanley Kirkpatrick, New York's police commissioner, he had got information from him. But the tone of the man's voice was cold and hostile now.

"It leads up to this," he said with precise, and inimical tones. "There are no bodies in the house and no trail but your own. You are going to be held with your man Jackson until the mystery of Miss Beach's disappearance is cleared up."

Wentworth said flatly: "Then it will never be cleared up."

"What do you mean?" Reed's temper was rising. Wentworth smiled slightly, thrust himself up from the blankets. Reed took a short stride forward so that he stood directly over him, and

Wentworth held his brittle black eyes with his own, as he reached out his left arm and jerked the chief's legs out from under him! **REED WENT** down with a choked cry. His head struck a metal handle on the wall and he went limp. Wentworth's hand shot to the chief's hip, caught a revolver free and leveled it at the intern.

"Get Jackson in here," said Wentworth quietly. The intern opened his mouth to speak and his teeth clicked with a small chattering sound. "I c-c-can't. The p-p-police won't let him g-g-go."

"His head needs attention," said Wentworth, "and Chief Reed says it's O.K. Get going."

The intern jerked his head in a nervous nod, turned toward the rear door.

Wentworth flung a swift glance about. The sides of the ambulance were solid, unbroken by windows except beside the driver's seat. A narrow door connected the back compartment with the front. He heard the intern's voice ring out, clear and authoritative:

"Bring that man here. Chief Reed says it's O.K." Wentworth got up on his good knee and, dragging his left leg behind him, crawled up behind the intern. He saw Jackson coming heavily toward the ambulance. One policeman was shoving him along with a hand on his shoulder. Jackson's head wore a white bandage and hung heavily. His feet stumbled.

When the two reached the ambulance, the intern stepped aside to let Jackson enter. The cop stared beyond him, and his mouth sagged open. Wentworth leveled the revolver at his belly and said coldly, "Keep quiet and get in here! Jackson, get in."

Jackson's head came up slowly, but he was smiling and his eyes were alert. It was obvious he had been shamming for the benefit of the police. He reeled. "Carry me in," he said in the cop's ear, and Wentworth grinned approval. That would keep both the policeman's hands busy, keep him from thinking himself out of his funk. Laboriously, the cop lifted Jackson heavily into the ambulance and scrambled in himself.

"All right, Doctor," said Wentworth. "Get your driver—call him—and get away from here fast. If police try to stop you, just yell something about 'Chief Reed.'"

"Say!" spluttered the cop, "You ain't a-gonna...."

"Gag him, Jackson," said Wentworth carelessly.

"Better tie up the chief, too."

He moved laboriously forward with the intern, saw a policeman striding toward the ambulance suspiciously.

"Never mind the driver," said Wentworth quietly.

"Drive it yourself."

The intern threw a white look over his shoulder at the jab of the gun in his ribs, then wordlessly squeezed through the narrow door and behind the wheel.

"Hey!" the cop yelled.

The intern kicked the starter and, the gun grinding in his ribs again, called back, "Chief Reed's in a hurry."

The cop hesitated. The ambulance lurched forward. Then the policeman caught sight of Wentworth behind the driver, threw up his gun and—the side of the ambulance cut off further vision.

No sound of a shot came to Wentworth, however, and the ambulance, gathering speed, swung around a corner at his order. Probably the cop still was uncertain about the status of the police chief. But there would be pursuit....

"Through, Jackson?" he called back, and the ex-sergeant spoke close to him. "Sure, there wasn't any trouble."

"Fine," said Wentworth. "Get over there and take the wheel from this lad. He's a good doctor, but what we want now is a good driver."

JACKSON GRINNED, squeezed through the door and, standing up, steered the ambulance while the intern eased out from behind the wheel. Then Jackson dropped into place, and the motor sang a new song, a deep roaring song.

Wentworth motioned the intern inside with the gun, placed him seated across the ambulance from himself and they stayed like that silently while the car did stunts. Fifteen minutes of that and the ambulance motor became quieter, less frantic.

"O.K.," Jackson sang out. "Now where?"

"Find an alley, and park there," Wentworth called.

At his orders, the intern stretched out face down and Wentworth bound his wrists with adhesive tape. Then Jackson, the intern's visored white cap on his head and with Wentworth leaning on his arm, moved leisurely to a taxi that took them to a second hand clothing store, then to the Hotel Grant. Wentworth paid in advance for one day and in the room rapidly went to work to alter his and Jackson's appearance. The clothing helped, and the compact emergency makeup kit that Wentworth always carried did the rest.

49

Skillful padding gave Jackson a paunch to match his height and breadth. The wide jaws were hard to mask, but a day-old silvery beard helped. He silvered Jackson's hair with powder. The bandage was removed.

The entire time he worked, Jackson's eyes were steadily upon Wentworth's pain-thinned face. Jackson had never been in the secret of the Spider's activities. It was not that Wentworth did not trust him, not that he hadn't used him on occasion when the revelation of his secret identity was not involved. It was merely that he wished to keep the circle of those who were in the know as small as possible. As he worked swiftly over the chauffeur's face, he felt the man's eyes on his. He was conscious of an alert questioning.

"We could not wait, Jackson, to argue with the police," he said. "I could have established our innocence in time, but time is precious. If Miss Beach is to be rescued, we must act at once."

"That's right, sir," said Jackson quietly. "Look, Major, don't you tell me a thing, sir. Just tell me what you want done, and I'll do it."

The eyes of the two men met squarely and a faint smile played across Wentworth's fine lips. "And that means, Sergeant?"

Jackson hesitated. "Just that, sir, begging the major's pardon. If the major will give the objective…."

Wentworth's eyes grew kindly. "You'll be better able to take the objective, sergeant, if you understand what's involved." He explained briefly then the background of the kidnaping of Ann Beach. "The best way to clear ourselves, Jackson, will be to find and release her and get her confirmation of the story."

"And what are the major's orders?" Jackson's face was expressionless.

Wentworth took out his wallet and peeled off bills. "Get a dog that can follow a scent unfailingly. A trained police dog would be best. Take him to the Beach home and give him a sniff of creosote, then take him out in the street, and he should pick up the trail. I threw a bucket of creosote on top of the kidnapers' car as they went away. The drops falling off should make a trail.

"I don't expect the dog will be able to lead you more than a few miles but if the kidnapers are still in town, that should be enough. If, on the other hand, they take a road out of town, it will last long enough to indicate the route they're following. When the dog has taken you to the end of the trail, phone me at the Stagler Hotel. Ask for Carson Haggard."

Wentworth handed Jackson Chief Reed's revolver.

"I won't forget this, Jackson," Wentworth said and held out his hand.

Jackson grinned. "Hell, I want a crack at those mugs that kidnaped Miss Beach."

He saluted and marched out. "And, Jackson," Wentworth called after him. "Don't walk so fast. Remember, you're an old man now."

IT WAS ten minutes later that Wentworth, his face transformed now by thin hard rubber plates so that his cheeks were plump and his nostrils widened—he had painted on thin, spider-web veins that gave his nose a purplish cast like that of a sufferer from chronic pulmonary trouble—left the room.

Closing the door, he moved slowly down the hall. Since he could not eliminate the limp, he pretended a muscular affliction of both legs, walking stiffly. The elevator toward which he walked flung open with a dull clang and three men came out fast. Two wore police uniforms. The third was Chief Reed, fairly bouncing with anger, his mustache bristling.

Wentworth stared at them dully, like a man too long ill to be interested much in anything. He moved on heavily with his dragging feet. Reed's quick black eyes flashed over him and beyond. He quick-stepped on, then, opposite Wentworth, he whirled and struck out violently with his fist. He struck not at Wentworth's jaw, but directly at his wounded thigh!

The blow was hard and it gouged cruelly into the already tormented wound. A wave of brain-blackening pain swept up over Wentworth. He fought grimly for control, knowing that Chief Reed suspected his identity, knowing that there was no chance for escape by rapid flight because of his wound, knowing that he must be free or city and state would fall under the dominion of the Devil and his disintegrating explosive!

CHAPTER 7
A DESPERATE TRICK

WENTWORTH STIFFENED his tortured body against the wall. But there was no fear in his face or posture. He glared at Chief Reed furiously.

"You blundering fool!" he rasped. "Why don't you look where

you're going? You doddering idiot! You imbecile! Coming slamming down the hall without regard for anyone."

"Keep quiet, you old fool!" a cop ordered gruffly. "Keep quiet, eh! Old fool, am I!" Wentworth exploded. His voice was creaky with old age, but it was penetrating and full of choler. "That's the way it is with you cops. Because you got uniforms and brass buttons...."

Reed was standing back, studying him with narrowed eyes. Wentworth moved toward him on his bent afflicted legs, shaking a trembling fist under his nose, a fist that Wentworth had not failed to disguise with age as he had the rest of his body.

One policeman caught Wentworth by the shoulder. "Get back!" the man ordered. "That's Chief Reed." Wentworth let himself be thrust back as if he were feeble.

He leaned back against the wall. His chest heaved. He was, apparently, a man in the grasp of the pulmonary ailment that had spread broken, empurpled veins over his nose.

"I don't care if he's the governor himself," he shrilled. "People got some rights. You can't go around knocking folks about like that. There's a justice...."

Heads were thrust out of doors. An elevator discharged two men and a woman and the operator heard the sounds of altercation and slammed the doors. Reed was still watching suspiciously. How far could Wentworth carry this bluff? But he knew. He must make Reed leave the scene or else force Reed to expel him from the hall.

He shook his fists again, growing hoarse with his ravings. "You little whippersnapper!" he shouted. "Think because you're

53

chief of police you've got a right to go around knocking into people who are old and sick." He appealed to the people about him, to those who thrust their heads out of doorways. "This is what causes revolutions," he declaimed.

"For gosh sake, Chief," one of the cops appealed, "let me sock him and get out of here."

Wentworth leveled a trembling finger at him.

"Go on and hit me! Go on! I'll sue the city for a million dollars. I'll get a bill in the legislature...."

Reed sniffed, jerked his shoulders in a shrug and pelted on up the hall. Wentworth staggered after him on bent, disabled legs, shaking his fist and hurling curses. "I'll have the law on you for this. I'll see my lawyer...."

The elevator door jerked open again, and the manager strode down the hall, his palms pushing the air soothingly before him. "Everything is all right. Everything is quite all right," he assured

everyone. He reached Wentworth's side and touched him on the shoulder. Wentworth whirled on him, berated him for siding with the authorities, called him a coward, and allowed himself to be propelled into the elevator where he muttered himself into silence. A taxi shot him away.

HE MADE a series of cab changes then, stopping at stores to get a suitcase and clothing and finally—after eating and changing his disguise in the restaurant wash room—emerged as a somewhat wan young man who wore a special high-heeled shoe on his left foot and limped heavily. His suit was such a light gray as Wentworth himself would never have worn, somewhat ill-fitting across the shoulders. His face was pale and his eyes seemed large because of the smudged mauve shadows beneath them. When he smiled, yellowish buck teeth showed like a squirrel's. In this guise, he went to the Stagler Hotel in a cab and registered as Carson Haggard. Jackson had not called....

Disappointed, he left his newly purchased suitcase in his room and, face drawn, went back to the street. He must see Nita at once and warn her that Ram Singh might be dangerous because he had fallen prey to the Devil and his drugs.

From a drugstore he phoned her hotel and soon saw her drive up to the corner in a rented coupé. He made a secret sign to her as she walked briskly into the store.

"Why, Mr. Haggard," she exclaimed. "I didn't recognize you at first!" She held out a neatly gloved hand, her blue eyes laughing at him beneath the sweep of her off-the-face bangkok. The dress was simple, of pale lavender silk, and lent a soft glow to the superb whiteness of her throat.

Wentworth bowed jerkily as if not quite used to such gallantry and limped away beside her to the car. Immediately Nita was grave, inspecting the drawn paleness of his face. He showed his false yellowish teeth in a smile.

"Oh, Dick! Those horrible teeth!" Nita shuddered, and Wentworth removed them, laughing. They gazed deeply into each other's eyes. Dick's, cool and gray, were slightly smiling, Nita's solemn and worried.

"Ram Singh said you were wounded," she accused him.

Wentworth waved a hand. "I'm not disabled.

Listen, Nita dear, in some way the purchase of the parks is paramount with this gang. Can you find out why?"

"Who knows?"

"Probably Delancey Howard," Wentworth told her. "He's the man who's handling the entire deal, though I'm not convinced he's the head of it."

Nita spun the car off Berkeley into Lake Drive past the rising elegance of apartment houses and frowned at the road. "Delancey Howard," she repeated. "Yes, it must be the same one I met at… No matter. I'll do my best, Dick."

Wentworth put his arm lightly about her shoulders. "No one could ask more, darling."

When he had warned her of Ram Singh's condition and she had promised to do her best with Delancey Howard, he took a taxi to the Capitol and made his halting way up the broad steps into the dim arch of the echoing hallway. In the ante-room of the governor's offices, he drew out a long paper he had prepared with columns of names from the telephone directory and insisted that the petition—so he called it—be presented in person to the governor.

After a long delay, he succeeded in entering the executive office to find the governor seated behind a large, flat-topped desk of hand-carved mahogany. He nodded pleasantly, a man of middle-age, his head bald and gleaming except for a fringe of mouse-colored hair, his mouth tight and aggressive beneath an intelligent nose, glittering, rimless glasses.

"I can give you but a few minutes," he said. "These are busy days."

WENTWORTH LIMPED up to the desk, holding the petition in his hands.

"They're going to become even busier," he said quietly. "Governor, the park bill must be defeated."

The governor waved a thick, short-fingered hand in a choppy gesture. "You know I'm fighting it."

"That's not enough." Wentworth shook his head slowly. "The men who murdered Senator Beach and kidnaped his daughter are behind the purchase."

The governor said emphatically, "That's ridiculous!"

Wentworth tapped a stiff fore-finger on the edge of the desk. "That's only the beginning," he declared. "This gang is planning wholesale looting of cities with that explosive. And the purchase of the park lands is vital to their plot."

The governor was eyeing him keenly. He had round black eyes that had a habit of fixed regard which his glasses emphasized. Their roundness was slightly tightened now.

"How do you know these things?" he asked. Wentworth

shook his head. "If I tell you how I know," baring those false buck teeth of his with a slight smile, "you must guarantee me unhindered exit from the building."

A slow frown gathered above the governor's narrowing eyes.

"Keep your hands away from those buttons," Wentworth ordered. It was said deferentially, almost apologetically, yet there was a force in his voice that drove the governor's hand away from that neat row of white bell buttons.

A phone buzzed faintly. "Be careful," Wentworth warned; and the governor, eyes steadily on his, lifted the instrument to his ear. "Yes... Show him in." He hung up, smiling faintly. "I have a vague idea that I'm being threatened," he said dryly. "It is an experience, but don't think you could get away with any violence. The building is too closely guarded."

Wentworth permitted himself a slight smile also. "You are mistaken about being threatened, Governor," he said calmly. "You asked for information, and I told you how you could obtain it. That was all."

The door opened behind him. The governor, without looking toward the door, said, "Come in, Howard."

The agent of the conspirators walked into the office!

CHAPTER 8
THE ROAD TO HELL

WENTWORTH STEPPED a little to one side so that he kept both men in view. Delancey Howard came forward on swift, aggressive feet, a wedge of a man tapering from squared wide shoulders to ridiculously small and exquisite feet, his triangular build emphasized by frock coat and gray striped trousers. A cherubic smile on his full pink cheeks, he bowed faultlessly and the light gleamed on hair that was sleekly blond.

"I'm so sorry," he said. His voice was unctuous and mocking.

"Why do you want the park lands, Howard?"

Wentworth demanded. "The bill guarantees that they will be held forever inviolate as parks and open to the public. Apparently all you get out of it is a few concessions."

Howard rubbed pink palms together. "My client is a philanthropist," he said in the same tone. "He will improve the parks as the state could not afford in fifty years."

"For the concessions?"

Howard, still smiling cheerfully, nodded. "For the concessions."

Wentworth's smile matched his own. "Howard, you're a liar." The man stiffened, spluttering, but Wentworth pushed on. "Either you're dumb, which I doubt, or you are a deliberate criminal, which is what you appear to be."

Howard's mounting belligerence left him almost at once and he shrugged, beaming more cheerfully than ever. "These cranks...." The governor was watching them both with speculative eyes.

Wentworth's face was bitter, his eyes hard. "The Devil, Mr. Howard."

A momentary tightening of the man's eyes answered that, and Wentworth rapped out "The Devil is behind this. He needs the park lands because without them he can't make his explosive. The explosive that killed Senator Beach, the explosive he intends to use to loot whole cities and murder those who stand in his way!"

Howard's face had become utterly impassive now, a smiling mask that betrayed nothing of what went on in the lawyer's shrewd mind. Wentworth was guessing wildly, but the man's very lack of reaction to what he said indicated he might have struck on the truth. The lawyer lifted his shoulders at the governor, smiling, always smiling. He executed another suave bow.

"Cranks always talk religion. I'll come back some other time when the crank isn't here." He stalked out.

Wentworth faced the governor across his desk.

"It does sound like crank talk, Mr. Governor," he said directly. "But what man would have believed that these vast criminal organizations of recent months could have arisen—the men behind the Mad Hordes that ravaged the middle west with hydrophobia, the fearful crew of the Bloody Serpent...." *

The governor's face was kindly now. "Yes, yes, you are right,"

---

* AUTHOR'S NOTE: These titanic battles of the Spider against criminals who organized nation-wide slaughter by the horrid torture of hydrophobia germs for their personal profit; and against the racketeers who turned to narcotics and spread their poison throughout the land were recounted in the April and May issues of *The Spider Magazine* by Mr. Stockbridge. He called these crusades of the Spider, "The Mad Horde" and "Serpent of Destruction."

he said. "You'd better go home now and get a rest and don't read so many of those silly newspaper stories. Detective books late at night...."

Wentworth's face was grave. "It is the same old story. Men in power never realize the peril until it has them by the throat. They scoff at stories of international intrigue, of a powerful league of criminals. Man, the stories you read in magazines and newspapers are not half the truth! Every day the Underworld concocts some new and horrible menace against humanity, something that must be suppressed before it is fairly organized else civilization would crumble. Half of them never become public knowledge."

"Yes, yes," said the governor, "doubtless you are right. Would you mind if I excused myself now? I have a great deal to do...."

Wentworth shook his head slowly. He could not blame the governor overmuch. Skepticism is bred by higher politics. If the Spider had not known these things, if he were a comfortable merchant or a clerk living in the midst of his suburban family, he, too, would scoff at these perils. They made entertaining newspaper reading, or when some deep-probing searcher after truth turned the things he knew into fiction because otherwise they could never gain print, they furnished an evening's thrill. But to the public, too, these truths seemed unbelievable.

Wentworth studied the man before him, skimming through papers now. What more could he do to make the governor realize the menace? The state's chief executive looked up with a frown.

"I've asked you to go," he said.

Wentworth nodded quietly. "I'm going, Mr. Governor. I know already that you are fighting the bill strongly. When the bombings and the lootings begin, remember what I have said—that the men behind the park bill are behind that, too."

HE BOWED and limped to the door, feeling the governor's curious gaze on his back. Delancey Howard smiled benignly on him in the anteroom and rose to enter the office. Wentworth moved on down the long echoing hall and out into the glare of the late afternoon sunlight. Newsboys were scampering along the street, shouting extras, and their excited cries stabbed cold horror into Wentworth's breast. Had the Devil already struck?

"Hey! Boy!" he called, seized a paper. His hands were white with the tension of his grip. The full weight of the Devil's fearful weapon had been crashed into the face of humanity!

Bloomington, New York, had been laid waste, not in one fell swoop, but systematically. In a simultaneous blast that had rocked the country for miles around, police stations, electric plants, radio and telephone exchanges had been blown into the dust! And with those buildings had perished some four hundred persons. And the city was being looted, house by house, bank by bank!

As he skimmed through the paragraphs, standing in shocked immobility upon the steps of the capitol, four men alighted at the corner from a limousine that remained parked there. They strolled separately toward Wentworth. He read on… The ragged men who fringed every city of the east now with their debris-built huts were blamed by the paper. They had joined in the looting, had robbed stores of food and clothing, stripped

63

the houses of the terrified and fleeing residents, committed unnameable crimes. Absolute anarchy reigned.

The reports were still fragmentary. These were undoubtedly the first flashes. The full horror, Wentworth knew, would reveal that banks and all spots of wealth had been stripped by the gangs while the unemployed had been used to spread terror. The governor must be getting the first reports now. Undoubtedly he was ordering out troops. But the crippled communications, the blasted telephone offices, would have prevented help until the looting had been completed. This news was hours late. The soldiers would find only the ragged men of the huts who would bear the brunt of the reprisals, who would be blamed for the entire atrocity while the Devil and his crew escaped.

Burning with anger, his eyes gray flame, Wentworth turned to stalk back to the governor's office, to fling this story in his face as proof of what he had claimed—and looked into a pair of mocking eyes. A man behind him showed a gun concealed in his hand, then put that hand in his pocket.

He said, "Turn around and walk down the steps like a nice boy."

Wentworth looked swiftly to right and left. A man stood on each side. Not close enough to seize, but close enough so that their bullets could not miss. Yet there was nothing to betray them to the casual eye.

"Turn around and go down the steps," the first man repeated coldly.

Wentworth, moving even more awkwardly than usual on his disabled leg, limped down the broad steps. There was a fourth gunman on the sidewalk. Up near the corner, the limousine purred into motion, slid to the curb. With four guns centering on him, one from a man who entered the car ahead of him, three from behind, Wentworth climbed laboriously to the back seat and dropped into the cushions.

"Kind of you gentlemen," he murmured. "I was wondering if I had enough money to taxi to my hotel."

THREE OF the gunmen covered him. The fourth sauntered into the Capitol, and the car slid forward. Wentworth looked over the men. One sat on his left, the other two were straddling the kick seats, guns in hand. The chauffeur wore livery.

The limousine turned north at the corner of the Capitol and loafed along obeying the traffic lights lazily. They were in no hurry now. They had their man—helpless. Wentworth unbuttoned his coat slowly, the eyes of the gangsters following every movement of his fingers. He smiled at them. "You don't mind if I smoke?"

Silence to that, but the eyes still watched as he slid his platinum and black enamel cigarette case from his pocket, snapped it open and offered it around.

But his captors all refused at the stiff negative shake of their leader's head. His eyes were mocking.

"No tricks, mister."

Wentworth raised his brows, "Oh, I assure you!"

He breathed out blue smoke. "May I ask where this ride will terminate?"

"Uh-huh."

"Where?"

"In hell."

Wentworth lifted his pointed, always mocking brows and smiled slightly. "Does that mean I'm going to see the Devil? Or did you mean an actual hell?"

The leader cursed cheerfully. "You're talking too much. You'll find out soon enough."

Wentworth lit another cigarette. There were two thin tubes of white paper in that case which were contained in a small secret compartment that a touch would open. One held a thin steel pipette and in it was a narcotic dart. If he puffed through the cigarette the dart would penetrate a man's flesh and within a space of seconds that man would be unconscious. Other such darts were in his cigarette lighter.

The other apparent cigarette, after it had burned perhaps a quarter of its length, would release a swiftly expanding narcotic gas. Either one of these weapons, or perhaps the two together, would win a probable release from this trap. But were they bound for a visit to the Devil? If they were, Wentworth would delay his escape until such time as he had located the Devil's headquarters.

The car droned on, turned left onto the Lake Drive and began to pick up speed. The man on his left screwed about in his seat, and Wentworth felt a jab of pain in his throat. He saw the hypodermic needle withdrawn.

After a moment of shock, he began to smile quietly. If they were bothering to dope him, he was bound for a mortal hell, the lair of the Devil-face fiend behind the looting of Bloomington! He closed his eyes and in two minutes was making gentle snoring sounds.

CHAPTER 9
CAVERN OF HORROR

WHEN WENTWORTH regained his senses, night was black about them. From the rise and twist of the road beneath the tunneling headlights, he knew they were in the hill country. It would be easy to overcome these men now, while they did not know he had regained consciousness. But he only yawned, opened his eyes and looked curiously about him. Moving his body a little, he felt his cigarette case and wallet.

Five minutes later the car turned sharply right and within fifty feet was burrowing through trees that arched completely over the road. The blackness of midnight was here and the headlights swept up and down with the slow jouncing of the machine, showing the thick green foliage crowding close on either side. A half hour of that and they eased to a halt beside a pile of raw yellow earth. The damp smell of it drifted in warmly on the night breeze as the car door was flung wide. A dome light in the ceiling popped on whitely and, as before, two men stood outside with leveled guns and the third, behind him, kept him carefully covered.

Wentworth maneuvered his stiff leg out first.

His head was throbbing dully from the dope as he followed the path of the headlights around the mud heap. Two flashlights showed him the way up a slippery, narrow path, then flickered over the low and narrow mouth of a cave. The path led straight into it and the guns urged Wentworth on.

So this was the entrance to hell! He smiled wryly and was forced to bend far forward to enter. Once inside, he found flickering oil flares along the walls and the flashlights were put out. The close arch of stone above his head made the whisper of their feet a gigantic cobra's hiss and the man spoke, when at all, in low, echoing mumbles.

The reverberations told Wentworth that they were approaching a large open chamber. "Wait a minute," the leader warned. "Minute… minute," said the echoes.

He flashed the light ahead and showed two planks nailed to a log. The log floated in water that cast back a hundred reflections and something darted away beneath the surface with a ripple. He lifted the beam of the torch. It rolled back the darkness, but as far as the light showed, there was a continuation of those two planks off across black water.

To either side of them the light glittered on spires and stalagmites of crystal that were like drooping Spanish moss. They cast weird shadows….

A thrust between his shoulder blades sent Wentworth stumbling out on the boards.

He dragged his aching leg and moved slowly out along the planks. They dipped, smacking the water at each tread, but presently they were firmer and Wentworth reached a float, saw a series of such floats supporting the boards—a pontoon bridge.

As he entered the second span, he heard the planks behind

him slapping and saw the leader of the gang start out also upon the bridge. Wentworth inched on. Obviously the tunnel behind was the only entrance to this cavern that the men knew; otherwise they would not have sent him ahead. That tunnel had been chiseled out by men recently. This cavern was of the vast architecture of nature.

For more than half a mile, Wentworth estimated, they continued their slow advance across the slippery, wet planks, sometimes half afloat, sometimes letting water wash over their shoe soles. Finally he made out far ahead the minute gleams of crystal and presently the hacked-out mouth of another tunnel. He turned his head about.

"You know I always heard the lakes of hell were of fire and brimstone," he said. "Brimstone," muttered a near echo. "Brimstone," whispered one afar.

He looked downward into the black water and minute points of red fire glowed in it, moving red points of fire that whirled and danced and spun in weird rhythmic figures.

"Hurry!" the gangster behind shouted. "Hurry! Hurry. The fire eyes!"

BEHIND CAME the excited clatter of feet on the boards. They dipped beneath Wentworth's feet, making him lurch, arms swinging wildly for balance. He shuffled on for the shore. The echoes were like a thousand men now, howling in fear. Smiling grimly, Wentworth stretched a hand out to the wall ahead, catching the long sharp point of a stalagmite which thrust upward near the walk. He jerked and the brittle stuff snapped.

The Devil leapt in among
the deadly eels.

Reaching the shore, he spun and whirling it once about his head, sent it hurtling along the line of the boards.

It struck the first man full in the chest. He threw up his hands with a strangled cry. His flashlight flew from his clutch and circled weirdly upward, spattering light over a sparkling wealth of crystal above and below. By its light, Wentworth saw the man pitch toward the black waters and heard his shriek of fear end in a splash. The spots of fire darted toward him while he lathered the lake with his struggles and raised a thousand tortured echoes with his cries.

The shouts of the others were drowned in his frantic fear. Wentworth laughed softly and, crouching within the entrance of the tunnel, snapped off another stalagmite that the centuries had labored to build. Once more he whirled and loosed the spear-shaped stone but this time he threw low along the surface of the boards in case the other men should have sought safety by crouching down.

A scream rewarded his throw and he sent three more of the strange missiles sizzling along the boards. He heard shouts behind him now. They were faint against the clamor of the men struggling in the water of the subterranean lake. Their shrieks cut off sharply with a gurgling of drowning. It seemed queer to hear the echoes of their dying cries after the men were dead....

But what were those queer sparks of fire that they feared so mortally? But the shouts were echoing behind him now. He heard the beat of feet, saw the dancing gleam of electric torches.

Wentworth stepped cautiously out on the boards, throwing the pencil beam of his small pocket light ahead of him. A slimy, snake-like body lay across his path. It was three inches through and its head and tail were sunk beneath the water on opposite sides of the plank walk.

With caution he might pass that danger in his path, but with this injured leg, he stood small chance of crossing the pontoon bridge before the men behind overtook him. He glanced swiftly to his right along the wall, reached out to the side of the tunnel and grasped the thick bases of two crystal pinnacles. Using his arms more than his legs, he drew himself upward until he could get his good foot upon the pedestal of a column he had snapped off. From there, he made his way slowly up a slope steepled with the stony growth as with trees. He found a sink between two enormous spires and eased into it.

The flicker of lights danced out on black water and a group of men poured out into the small shelf that formed its lip and halted there. They sent their lights searching over the waters, spotted the snakelike thing across the walkway and two floating hats—and that was all. The men did not go out on the pontoon bridge to investigate. They stood for a long time looking out over the black lake with its whirling red sparks, muttering words that the echoes garbled too much for Wentworth to understand. Then slowly they went back down the tunnel from which they had come.

Wentworth waited fifteen minutes, eased his slow way back to the ledge of stone and turned into the tunnel behind the men who had vanished.

He was unarmed, except for his wits, but—the smile was sinister now on the lips of the Spider—that armament had proved more than sufficient for many criminals before now! He thrust always his left foot forward, feeling his way while his right supported his weight. His progress was soundless as the shadows....

Suddenly, without warning, a terrific clangor of bells jangled into the silence! Instantly lights sprang up all about him, lights and men. Dazzling beams glared into his eyes and guns thrust their ugly muzzles toward him.

"Welcome to Hell!" a man cried mockingly, the resonant taunting voice of the Devil!

CHAPTER 10
THE LAKE OF DEATH

WENTWORTH GRINNED in a semblance of a frightened grimace, showing the yellowish, buck teeth of Carson Haggard. He began to back away from the menace of those guns. But the guns were behind him, too.

"Come, come," said the Devil, still invisible, "this pretense of fear will not work. For you see, you limp with the left leg and it so happens that I put a bullet through the left leg of a gentleman known as the Spider. It will only be necessary to rip your trouser leg...."

Wentworth ceased his retreat, straightened out of the silly crouch which he had hoped might throw these men off guard, and, lifting a hand, casually removed the false teeth.

"I am glad these are no longer necessary," he said. "They're rather uncomfortable. And you know my identity, don't you,

M'sieu' Devil, because I thought such a simple thing as a bullet had killed you and made a phone call identifying myself in your presence."

The Devil was mocking as always, "Glad to be of some small assistance to you, Mr. Spider."

As he spoke, a man moved along the wall with a flaming torch. The weird red fire of oil wicks smoked upward in the darkness and showed the Devil seated upon a high-backed chair built crudely of undressed wood. The men had waited so for Wentworth to walk into the trap, waited with an exact understanding of the Spider's mental processes—knowing that he would not quit the search when he seemed so close to the goal. It was such a trap as the Spider himself might have set.

Wentworth looked slowly about the place where he was prisoner, a square chamber chiseled out of rock. Yet it had not a modern look. It might have been fashioned a hundred, two hundred years ago. Only that tunnel beyond the lake was new. The red glare of the torch flames, the red robe that the Devil wore seemed as artificial as an opera set, but there was no disguising the seriousness of his plight.

"I had you brought here only to make sure that you would die, Spider," he said slowly. "Others have attempted to kill you and you seemed to bear a charmed life. I shall personally witness your execution." He peered at Wentworth, seeking some sign of weakness. But there was none. The calm, contemptuous eyes of the Spider met his without flinching. There was even a light amusement about the finely chiseled lips.

Wentworth said, "I have marked you for death, Devil." He

thrust out a pointing finger. "Why do you paint over my seal? Do you fear that your men will lose faith in you if they know that you wear the red brand of the Spider on your forehead?"

The men about them shuffled uneasily again.

They glanced at one another and a few dared to lift their eyes curiously to the forehead of the Devil. Nothing showed there, but this prisoner had mentioned paint....

"You lived under that seal once, Devil," Wentworth taunted, "but it has doomed you. It means your death as surely as...."

"You die tonight!" the Devil snapped out. He jerked to his feet, stabbing a pointing finger at Wentworth, his arm draped with the red robe. "You die tonight, Spider, but first I want you to know a few things to keep you from resting too easily in your grave—" he flung back his head and laughed—"and what a grave it will be, Spider!"

He stared gloatingly at the man who stood so calmly before him. "Today, in Bloomington, we took nearly a million dollars," he said. "Schenectady and Buffalo are next. And next Friday— that's four days from now when our parks bill is passed—we blow up the governor in his office and rape Albany. The lieutenant governor will sign the bill. When we have paralyzed the state, New York City itself shall fall before us." His voice had become a chant of sinister menace now. "The entire nation cannot stand against us."

Wentworth smiled and shook his head as if marveling at the madness of the other. "All those things might well happen," he said gravely, "but for one thing."

THE DEVIL snorted. "Nothing can stop me," he declaimed.

Wentworth nodded his head slowly, portentously. "One thing can stop you," he said, "one thing. Your death. And already the Spider's doom is upon you. The seal is on your forehead! No, Devil, you will never achieve these things."

The Devil stabbed his draped, crimson clad arm toward the black tunnel behind Wentworth.

"Take him to the lake," he ordered, "and throw him in. After that, we shall see what comes of your boast, Mr. Spider." He whirled toward his men. "To the lake, I say!"

Over the men grouped there in that weird chamber far below the earth's surface, a shudder swept like a cold wind. Not one of them moved. The Devil threw back his head and laughed, a mocking cruel mirth.

"They are a little timid about the lake, Spider.

And they have reason to fear it." He took slow strides from his chair toward Wentworth, "Do you know what the snakes are, Spider?" It was a sneer.

Wentworth nodded, his expression unchanging. "Of course," he said. "It's some sort of gymnonotous fish, apparently *Electrophorus electricus,* although I never heard of an electric eel outside of Brazil before."

The Devil sneered. "Nevertheless, it will do no harm to go into a few details about the eel's delightful little habits. It will slide its slimy body against you in the black water and touch you ever so gently with its tail. You will go numb all over, shocked into paralysis, but you will still be conscious when you sink down, down, down through the black water to become carrion for them to feed upon!"

Wentworth ducked and smashed Howard in the face with the gun.

Wentworth let his smile widen slightly. "You're slightly melodramatic, Devil." His voice was matter of fact. "It will help some to know that I sent three of your men, as you so aptly put it, 'down, down, down' tonight." He glanced about him and abruptly he laughed, the flat chest laughter of the Spider. "Some others may go down, down, *down* with me!"

The Devil walked close and slapped him heavily in the face. Wentworth seized the striking wrist, whirled and thrust out

his foot and the Devil went down, slapping his head against the wall. Instantly Wentworth was upon him, groping for a pistol. He found it on the hip, snapped it upward covering the half-hearted attack that the circling men had begun.

"You," he indicated a man with the revolver, "tie all your friends." The man hung back, but Wentworth forced him to obey. When only that man and one other were still free, Wentworth halted the work and ordered, "Pick up the Devil."

The men hung back, but Wentworth's gun intimidated them and with the two carrying the Devil, he went as swiftly as his injured leg would permit down the black tunnel toward the walkway and the lake of the electric eels. The men bearing his prisoner moved reluctantly, but Wentworth goaded them with threats.

"Down, down, down," he chanted at them. "Death in the lake to the first man who falters."

On and on went the queer procession, the two in front carrying the Devil by his feet and shoulders, his red robe dangling; Wentworth limping behind with the light in his hand, a gun ever ready.

Presently its beam shot out into the black cavern of the lake and as they came nearer, they saw the red swimming sparks that were the eyes of those loathsome snake-like creatures with their bare, gleaming backs and their fearsome powers.

THE MEN hung back but Wentworth forced them out on the planks.

"The walkway won't hold but one at a time," the first man wailed, "and there's three of us."

Wentworth fired a bullet into the wood at the man's heel, gouging through the leather of his shoe. He surged forward, and the other followed. Wentworth stood back a little way, let them get a fifteen feet lead before he followed.

Each time the men ahead stepped, it was in water up to their ankles and on all sides swarmed the red eyes of the eels.

Now their slow procession had reached the middle of the long walkway. Wentworth, watching his prisoners ahead, shouted an abrupt warning:

"Look out! The Devil!" He lurched into a swift shuffle along the walkway.

His warning came too late. Even as the men became aware that the master they carried helplessly between them had recovered consciousness, the Devil thrust violently with his feet, struck a savage blow with his fist and propelled both his men into the water.

Their screams soared to the vault, terrible, throat-tearing shrieks of absolute terror. Once, twice, they sounded while the men floundered frantically to regain that narrow walkway which meant life. Then Wentworth saw one gangster stiffen, his eyes staring wide open, his mouth agape. Rigid as a board, he sank into the depths. The other death he did not see. He heard the cry choke off.

But the Devil had sprung upright upon the walkway, between him and the exit of this hell chamber. His evil face was twisted into a fierce grin in the glare of Wentworth's white torch. He jerked his hand to his hip, found no pistol.

Wentworth laughed mockingly. "I have your gun, Devil," he said. "Surrender at once, or I'll put a bullet through your leg and leave you to your gentle eels."

The Devil straightened slowly, raising his hands halfway. "Do you think you can kill the Devil?" he demanded. His laughter was as wild as a madman's. He leaped into the air. Wentworth threw up the gun, then hesitated.

For the Devil had leaped not at him, but sideways in a clean swift dive.

The Devil had dived in among the deadly electric eels!

CHAPTER 11
THE SPIDER IS SHOT

AN INVOLUNTARY cry pushed up into Wentworth's throat. He thrust the beam of his torch out over the black waters. The red sparks of death still swarmed there, making tight, eager circles in the darkness. Small waves zig-zagged the path of the light and made liquid lapping sounds against the walkway—but that was all. The Devil had vanished.

But though he had dived cleanly and swiftly in among the eels, there was no rush of those baleful eyes toward the spot. It was as if they knew that human monster was one of their own kind, a kindred killer straight out of hell, one too evil for them to touch. The thought chilled Wentworth, sent a cold prickle over his scalp....

Water broke with a furtive splash. It was on the opposite side of the walkway! Wentworth whirled, probed the blackness with his light, sent a whining bullet to seek the Devil. But the lead only zipped into the water. He saw the needle of spray jet upward in the far rim of his torch's ray, as the roar of the shot clapped back from the walls. But if the Devil had come up for air there, he had vanished again too quickly for a shot to find him.

For an instant, Wentworth stared out into the darkness,

straining his eyes against the ebony curtain that billowed close against him. He sent the ray questing back and forth across the glistening black water, then he turned and dragged his wounded leg on toward the far shore of this accursed underground lake. Without reinforcements he could do no more. The pain in his thigh had become a burning agony that left him weak and nauseated.

Although he was convinced that the hollow belly of this mountain held somewhere the secret of the Devil's devastating explosive, he must turn his back and flee. Once out, he could summon troops to storm this citadel of hell, overpower the Devil and his men and seize his fearful secret. If they struck promptly, they would avert the sack of Buffalo and Schenectady, the looting of Albany planned by the Devil.

Wearily he struggled on and at long last thrust out into the velvet night that seemed twilight in contrast with the thick blackness of that subterranean vault. Haltingly, he made his fumbling, foot-dragging way about the heap of yellow mud that marked the entrance. Then, without warning, the fiery blast of a gun split the night wide open.

Wentworth snapped a shot at the flash, and the sharp report of his own gun blended with another crashing discharge from the weapon of the outside guard. He knew a moment of awful blazing light that seemed to sear his skull, then slumped down heavily against the pile of yellow earth.

For long minutes he lay there unmoving, then his arms began to twitch, his head to roll. Five minutes after the guard's bullet, scraping his skull, had hurled him to earth, he struggled up to his feet again, leaning against a small tree for support. He squeezed his throbbing temples between his palms. Hammers seemed to beat an Anvil Chorus upon his skull. He shook his head heavily, staggered toward the black woods ahead.

He stumbled upon the body of a man and his light showed a bullet hole through the chest. He stood staring down vaguely at the upturned face of the man he had killed even as that man's bullet had struck him down. Then Wentworth reeled on along a faint path. He blundered against an auto and rested there, leaning his hot forehead against the coolness of its metal. Ten minutes later he lifted his head, fumbled open the door and got behind the wheel.

The motor barked into life, the car lurched into a shrub-crashing turn and labored up the narrow woods road, yawed out onto the highway and drummed along at twenty-five miles an hour. This was not Wentworth's mode of driving. He did forty through the city, and on the road his car rarely dropped below sixty. But tonight he crawled. Through black woods he went, the machine swinging wide on curves, missing a half dozen collisions by the frantic swerves of other drivers, and finally labored out upon an open stretch. There was a twisting hill road ahead, and the auto took that at a faster pace—faster because Wentworth was sagging over the wheel, his foot heavy on the accelerator, his hands wooden on the wheel.

Up it swept. A sharp curve showed before the flashing lights, a sharp curve with a ravine beyond and a fence designed to stop cars—heavy wire cables strung between deep-set posts.

Wentworth's car went straight ahead. He was limp across the steering wheel now, his hands powerless at his sides.

The car hit the fence, bounced and slithered along the cables. Wentworth's foot bounced off the accelerator and the car jolted again into the cable, bent it perilously, jammed its nose against one of the deep set posts and stalled.

Wentworth did not stir. He was unconscious….

IT WAS four days later that Wentworth opened eyes sunken and dull in a worn face and stared up at the pug-nosed Irish girl that leaned over him, into blue Irish eyes that smiled beneath a jaunty probationer nurse's cap.

"Hello," said Wentworth faintly.

The nurse said, "Hi, big boy!" and left to call a doctor.

When he had come and felt Wentworth's pulse and asked questions, Wentworth sought an explanation of his presence here. He remembered having been kidnaped on the steps of the Capitol, he remembered the jab of the needle in the gangster's hand which had made him unconscious. After that nothing was clear. He had a vague idea that he had been in a vast cavern and that the cavern was horrible. He knew something vastly important had been said in that cavern, but what it was he did not know.

Wentworth struggled with his mind. He sought clues to where he had been by demanding the details of being brought to this hospital—it was the Cohoes Memorial he found—but the tourist who brought him had told only that he had found him on the side of a road. He had not said what road and had left hastily. Nothing to be learned there. Sweat beaded Wentworth's forehead as he fought to remember. Something important had been wiped from his brain as cleanly as with the sponge of death. He knew what had happened. His intense fatigue, coupled with the drug he had been given and his wounds, had caused a partial amnesia. He knew, and the knowledge terrified him. Try as he would, he could not recall that important something which, he feared, might mean life or death to thousands.

He could not recall that the Devil had taunted him with the fact that within four days he would blow up the governor and loot Albany! *He did not know that tomorrow was the day!*

FEVER MADE Wentworth's eyes dry and bright. He must leave this bed, speed back to Albany and take up the trail of the Devil again. Something horrible was impending, something that he knew and had forgotten…. He thrust himself up from the bed, demanding his clothing.

The doctor shook his head emphatically. "Not for a week, anyway. Probably two. You lost a lot of blood."

"Then get me a transfusion," Wentworth snapped.

The doctor frowned at him. "We already have done that. You're on the mend, but… No, no, Mr. Haggard, not for a week."

Wentworth shut his eyes to hide a momentary gleam of triumph. At least his false personality had survived. He had not the obstacle of being guarded by police.

When the doctor had gone, Wentworth pressed the button that summoned the nurse. When Irish eyes came back, he smiled up at her.

"I just wanted to see you again," he told her confidentially.

"Pooh!" said Irish eyes and walked out.

He continued to wheedle her all that day and it was around five o'clock when he made the proposal he knew she would have rejected hours ago, that she sell him back his wallet and his clothes—or just any clothes.

"Oh, but if you died," the nurse said gravely, "I'd be responsible."

"If you don't let me go, I'm going to die right here on your hands," Wentworth told her grimly and the nurse laughed and was defeated. She got him his bill fold and the white linen garb of an intern and he climbed into them stiffly, delighted to find that though his wounded leg was still sore, there was no longer the constant feverish throbbing that had tortured him before.

Wentworth gave the nurse two bills that made her gasp in protest—"But it isn't worth all that!" She held them out to him.

He closed her hand about them, shook his head, and eased out of the room. It took all his strength to stalk with a brisk business-like air down the hall. His limp was still pronounced, and the bandage on his head was a clean give-away, but he'd have to risk it. He made his way directly to Room 23 where medicine was kept. The nurse in charge looked up as he approached, recognized him for a stranger and gasped, her eyes on the head bandage. Wentworth smiled at her absently. The nurse hesitated. Wentworth stepped close and thrust the pocket of his jacket forward as if it contained a gun. His eyes held hers.

"Not a sound," he ordered curtly. "Give me a vial of scopo-malin or sodium amytol and a hypodermic." *

The girl's eyes were brown. They grew wide under his gaze and her head began to shake from side to side. "But—but I can't!"

"Quickly!"

"But...."

Wentworth took slow steps toward her, eyes commanding. "Quickly," he repeated, "or I'll use force." His voice was hard and his mouth tight. The nurse backed up, frightened, whirled to her medicine racks and handed over what Wentworth demanded with trembling hands. "It's—it's sodium amytol," she said.

He took it, shoved it into an inner pocket. "Now adhesive,"

---

* Author's Note: *Scopomalin* and *Sodium Amytol* are known as the "truth drugs." There are other substances which induce this semi-conscious state in which the mind is sufficiently awake for the person to speak, yet not enough aroused to permit the person to set up conscious obstacles to answering. This condition continues for only a short while, and the patient soon lapses into complete unconsciousness. But during the period of semi-consciousness the patient is incapable, because of a vast feeling of inertia and lassitude, of telling anything but the truth. This is based on the fact that the memory is a subconscious thing, while the deliberate falsification of a memory is an operation of the conscious mind. There has been widespread effort to introduce the use of these drugs in the handling of criminals, but the experimentation is still in its early stages, the dosage is still largely a matter of guess-work and an overdose may easily cause death.

he ordered. It took him ten minutes to bind her with the tape. He closed the door, limped down the hall and reached the street without interference. The evening coolness helped. He began to feel stronger. His wounded leg was limbering up and though still painful, allowed him to make good time.

COHOES IS about twenty miles from Albany, and Wentworth finally found a cab driver who for considerable sum would take him to the capital city. He still had not received Jackson's report on the trailing of the car that carried Ann Beach away; he did not know whether Nita had been able to accomplish anything toward learning the secret of the explosive or the criminals' hide-out from Delancey Howard. All his plans centered on the state capital. And he knew that the need for action was urgent.

Once there he contrived secretly, through back entrances, to reach his old room at the hotel Laurelton. He discarded the head bandage for a neatly taped patch and drew on over it a close red wig of bristling hair. He built a stubby mustache and, obtaining an extra automatic and money from his luggage, abandoned the rest of his things and stalked out of the hotel with a shoulder swaggering stride that his slight limp did not affect.

From a nearby restaurant he phoned the Hotel Stagler and, using Carson Haggard's tones, asked for a message.

"Yes, sir," the clerk told him. "Four days ago, a Mr. Jackson phoned that the place you were interested in was out on the road to Ausable Chasm. He didn't give the exact location."

"Thank you," said Wentworth. He was excited, but his voice did not betray it.

The Ausable Chasm road was the route the gangster car had followed before one of them had put him to sleep with a hypodermic. But he could not follow that road blindly. It would take a month to search the country along it for a cavern. If he could only get word from Nita. Perhaps she had learned something…. He snatched up the telephone again and called the hotel where Nita was staying. She was out and had left no message. That must wait then.

He went back to a table and ordered a steak with onions and French fries, had consomme while he waited and the waiter, shouting the order through a swing door into the kitchen, stopped by a creaky radio to fiddle with the dials. The loud-speaker squawked, boomed with vibration and picked up the quick staccato voice of a news broadcaster.

"Buffalo—" the voice began, "and now Schenectady has fallen prey to this savage horde of dynamiters and looters. Banks have been blown open, police stations and telephone exchanges blasted from the face of the earth. Hundreds, perhaps thousands, have been destroyed in these attacks of violence and pillage."

WENTWORTH CHECKED in his eating and stared out into the darkened street. Girls in summer dresses and groups of men sauntered past carelessly. Across the street, a motion picture theatre had long lines before it. The mazdas blinked out the message that they offered pictures of the Bloomington disaster. The voice was hammering on.

"… There wasn't anything left of the police stations and the brave men who make up the Buffalo and Schenectady police forces. The army of the unemployed, camped on the outskirts of these cities for weeks and months, marched into the streets, shouting hoarse threats, waving clubs and guns got from God knows where.

"The mob is ragged and unkempt. Their faces are matted with days and weeks of beard and their hands are dirty with black-rimmed fingernails. Their faces are not human. They are torn with the lust to kill and destroy *and loot*. They will murder and rob, and the women will be tortured. What power actuates these men? Who is their leader? Who has given them this titanic bomb which reduces all that it touches to dust?

"This speaker does not know. He only knows that the attacks are superlatively organized, that no word leaks out from the ravished cities until it is too late to stop their pillaging, and that when troops finally take the road to turn back the looting hordes, they find railroads and highways blown into nothingness by these strange and powerful bombs."

Wentworth had been listening intently, his food neglected before him. The waiter came and removed the soup, slapped down a greasy steak on the clothless, white porcelain table. "It's awful, ain't it?" he said nasally. "They ought to turn machine guns on them unemployed...."

Wentworth gestured him impatiently to silence, concentrating on the voice. He knew it, he was sure. It touched some responsive chord in his memory. But it was pouring out more words....

"This speaker does not know the authors of the crimes," the

speaker went on, "but Chief Reed, head of police in Albany, says that he does. In an interview today printed in the Albany *Press-Star*—I quote him directly—

" 'Yes, I know who is behind these crimes. He kidnaped Ann Beach and escaped the police by a trick. This was just after he had blown up Senator Beach with the same sort of explosive that he has used to devastate entire cities. That man masquerades as a wealthy man of family and leisure. His name is Richard Wentworth and we expect his arrest hourly. He limps badly in his left leg because of a bullet wound, and that will trap him.' "

Wentworth picked up eating implements slowly, began on the steak. His quick eyes kept close watch on the passing crowd. He was in disguise, but that tell-tale limp! His mouth closed in a grim line. He slapped down money on the table, jerked to his feet and moved swiftly toward the door.

The waiter stared after him, his eyes jerking from his limping figure to the radio. "A man who limps on his left leg…" the radio announcer was saying.

CHAPTER 12
NITA IS FALSE!

BUT WHILE he hesitated, Wentworth was gone.

The waiter dashed to a telephone and began yelling for police.

Wentworth hurried along the streets, lost himself in the crowds. His eyes were burning, and his suffering drawn face became even more taut with rage at these merciless and terrible massacres, at these killings for the mere sake of loot.

He went to a rental garage and ordered a small, swift coupé, planking down a deposit in lieu of identification. The radio was squawking here, too. The same voice pelted on. It related that the parks bill had been passed. The governor had not yet vetoed the bill. But he would send his veto message soon.

Something tugged at the back of Wentworth's brain. Something that he knew he should remember, but which would not reveal itself. Though he did not know, it was the hidden memory that the Devil had said passage of the bill would be the death knell of the governor and of Albany. But Wentworth did not remember!

Though he knew action, and immediate action, was necessary, he did not know how imminent was the peril that threatened the city, did not know that even now the cohorts of the Devil were planting their fiendish bombs about the city, awaiting only the signal of the master blast—the blast that would kill the governor.

That radio commentator's voice was familiar.

It reminded Wentworth of something he knew he should recall, but somehow the knowledge itself eluded him. As he listened, the man concluded his speech and the sing-song of the station announcer came over the air.

"You have just been listening to J. Osborne Pierce, in the News of the Day!"

J. Osborne Pierce. Wentworth smiled, remembering. That was the radio commentator he had met at the home of the

Beaches just before Ann had been kidnaped. But his smile was of short duration. Thinking of Pierce put him in mind of Ann. And anxiety for that brave and likable young woman straightened his lips grimly.

The car was delivered, and he slid behind the wheel and sent the machine speeding to Delancey Howard's apartment on Lake Drive. He parked a half block away and limped along the street, leaning lightly on a cane, a certain swaggering roll to his shoulders that fitted well with the bristling red mustache and out-thrust jaw he had assumed.

He strolled into the elaborate lobby, modishly angular and glittering with rich carpetings and chromium fixtures, entered the elevator and said, "Fifth."

At the fifth floor the door opened with a swish of compressed air and Wentworth limped to the apartment of Delancey Howard. His hand slipped to that compact kit of tools beneath his arm, and in a few moments' time his lockpick had clicked aside the last barrier to his entrance.

He eased in, let the door shut quietly behind him and stood peering quickly about. Gleaming mirrors with shaded lights colored the hall. The arched entrance to the room beyond was hung in soft blue velvet. Light came through the quiet voices, the small clatter of silver and china. Wentworth smiled, slipped on a black silk mask and drew the soft brim of his jaunty gray hat well down over his eyes.

Keeping the cane in his left hand, he stole forward, peering through the blue curtains. The lawyer's broad, formally clothed back was turned toward him and beyond him was the white gleam of an elaborately set table. Six candles in three-branch silver sticks gave the only light. Across the table from Howard, a cigarette dainty between her fingers, sat Nita van Sloan!

HER DRESS was black velvet and made the warmth of her shoulders clear and beautiful. She lifted the cigarette to her lips, let her arm fall across the corner of the table, and rested her chin on the back of her other hand. Smoke drifted from her red lips. Wentworth thought he had never seen her so beautiful, with her gleaming chestnut hair, and her blue eyes languorous, as she was now dining *a deux* with the man Wentworth suspected of being the Devil! There was no doubt at least that he had called the gangsters to kidnap him from the Capitol.

It was plain Nita had not as yet got the information she sought or she would not be here. But there was no time for further delay. He walked openly into the room.

"Sorry to intrude on so charming a *tête-à-tête,*" he said casually. "No, Howard, don't move suddenly. Just leave your hands upon the table. Am I wrong, or have the servants been dismissed for the evening?"

Howard's anger was deep in his throat, an inarticulate sound. He twisted his large head with its smoothly gleaming blond hair and looked at Wentworth with thick-lidded eyes. Nita had not moved. Her face mirrored fear and dread, and her blue eyes were wide.

"Sorry not to remove my hat in such company," Wentworth said, still casual, "but both my hands are occupied." One was on a gun in his pocket, the other on the cane braced against his leg.

Howard lurched to his feet, his thick-palmed hands clench-ing and opening slowly. Nita stood gripping the edge of the white table.

"Is this some trick, Del?" she demanded. "If it is, I don't see the point of it."

"It is not," said Howard. The oil was gone from his voice. It came out harshly. "Well, what do you want? Let's get it over with."

"In a hurry, Howard?" Wentworth drawled.

"Madame, I'll have to trouble you to tie your friend. He seems an impetuous gentleman." He flicked a humorous eye toward the stocky lawyer.

"I won't," Nita declared flatly. She put weight on her hands on the table so that she leaned forward slightly. Her rounded jaw was firm. Inwardly Wentworth applauded. She was acting out her part to perfection.

"Then," Wentworth drew out his automatic and held it slightly raised, "it will be necessary for me to put him *hors de combat* with a light tap of this." He took two cautious steps toward Howard.

Howard's small bright eyes were unwavering on Wentworth. When he made the second step, the lawyer sprang forward and kicked the cane. Wentworth jerked out of the way and slapped Howard down with the flat of the gun. He stood looking at him a moment, then pocketed the automatic and smiled at Nita.

"Nita, dear," he said. "I think I'd better tie you for the sake of appearances."

Nita said sharply, "Go away!" She backed away from the table.

Wentworth's smile faltered and, abruptly, Nita whirled and ran for the door behind her. He took two halting steps in pursuit, then shook his head in bewilderment and stood staring after her.

"Police!" he heard Nita call sharply. "Operator, send police to the home of Delancey Howard right away." She rattled off the address.

Wentworth uttered a low oath. Nita had betrayed him! Was it possible she had not recognized him? No, there was no chance of that. She had known him well enough, yet she had deliberately called the police!

Nita appeared suddenly in the doorway, a tense figure in black with gleaming shoulders and arms. She flung up a gun and fired!

CHAPTER 13
NIGHT ATTACK

WENTWORTH'S DUCK was instantaneous. At the first glimpse of gunmetal in Nita's hand he dived toward the elaborately set dinner table. He struck it hard and crashed it, with the candles, to the floor. The room was plunged in comparative darkness. But lights still glowed in the hall and he would be sharply silhouetted if he attempted to flee.

Although he moved with lightning rapidity, his mind was in a turmoil. Pictures of Nita betraying him to police, Nita firing on him with a revolver flashed madly through his brain. Above all living persons he had trusted this gorgeous girl, and now.... A flash of memory. Of course! It was the same drugs and hypnotism that had turned Ram Singh into an assassin!

Wentworth, moving awkwardly backward because of his wounded leg, made slow but silent progress to a door he had spotted to the left of the entrance curtains. He fingered it open and slipped through. A narrow pantry led to the kitchen. The window gave on a fire escape.

Wentworth threw wide the casement, tossed his hat to the floor, and secreted himself in a narrow closet that just held him and no more—a broom closet beside the kitchen sink. But, a close prisoner there, waiting for police to come and go, waiting for the chance that he must have to question Delancey Howard, Wentworth was prey to bitter doubts.

He could conceive of nothing but drugs and hypnotism that could cause Nita to betray him. But no one could have conceived of his visit and instructed her what to do. No drug could make her act except as subject to the will and commands of another. And the only other person in the room, Delancey Howard, had been unconscious when she had acted!

Wentworth closed his eyes wearily in the darkness. He could not doubt Nita. He would not believe she would ever turn on him despite the evidence of his own eyes. There must be some explanation.... Dimly, he heard the rumble of a man's voice, the quick excited contralto of Nita's. The voices kept on for a while and presently, the kitchen door opened noisily and lights went on.

Nita Van Sloan

"He went down the fire escape," said Delancey Howard heavily. "Lord! That beggar hit me a crack."

"I'm afraid I didn't hit him," said Nita. "I don't see any blood." Her voice was cold and filled with hate.

Wentworth heard the sound of Howard's hands patting gently on her shoulder. "No one expects a woman to shoot straight," he said magnanimously. "You were wonderful."

Their footsteps retreated, and soon police came and tramped

through the house. Half an hour after they had left, Nita's voice came faintly to Wentworth from the entrance hall. "Now, Del, you mustn't bother. A taxi will take me home all right. And if there's any trouble, I'll come right here even if it's four o'clock in the morning."

"That's right," said Howard. His voice was unctuous again. "I wish I could get rid of this fiendish headache. It's a shame to ruin the evening...."

The voices murmured into silence; the door clapped shut. Wentworth stood rigidly in his close closet. Her voice was so tender. God, *oh God!* Nita had turned false! A shudder seized him and left him weak.

Slowly the violence of emotion drained from him and, weak from pain and torment, he felt the slow heat of rage rise within him. He slid from the closet on soundless feet. Fury turned his eyes to gray flame.

Hand on the kitchen door, he paused. "Steady, Dick," he muttered, almost aloud. A sob pressed into his throat. He choked it back, used his finger tips to crack the door. The fingers trembled—the hand of the Spider trembled! There he stood, Delancey Howard, his broad back turned as he surveyed the mess the upset table had spilled upon his China rug. Wentworth's lips snarled back from his teeth. He opened the door and limped slowly forward, gun in hand.

"Sorry to trouble you twice in the same evening," he said suavely.

HOWARD WHIRLED with a frightened cry, started

toward the mantel on which lay the small revolver Nita had fired.

Wentworth said softly, "I wouldn't do that, Howard."

Howard stopped. There was a quiver in the lawyer's throat that was not all anger. There was fear in his heavy-lidded eyes, fear of this man who vanished when he was pursued and returned to harry when the pursuit had disappeared.

"Listen, Wentworth," he said hoarsely. "I know you and police know you, thanks to Miss van Sloan. If anything happens to me here tonight, you'll pay for it. Never doubt that."

Wentworth's lips lifted in a twisted smile beneath that stubbily artificial mustache. So Nita had told them his identity! Then the last shred of hope was gone. Definitely she had known him; deliberately she had fired upon him. Knowing who he was, she had called in police....

Wentworth laughed shortly, wildly. He hopped forward. Howard squealed, whirled. Instantly Wentworth was upon him. He whipped down with his gun, and the rotund lawyer ground his face into the floor.

Wentworth stood then with his chest heaving. It had been hard to make that blow light, hard to keep from striking to kill. His hand clenched the gun whitely.

He forced himself to pocket the automatic. He jerked his head savagely as if he would shake clear of that buzzing fury, then set swiftly to work. Once more he was the methodical, self-possessed Spider.

He took out the vial of drug from the hospital and filled the hypodermic needle. He jabbed it into Howard's throat and

101

pressed the plunger home. He glanced at his watch then, and bending over the man he sponged his forehead hard with a damp napkin from the table. Dirt came off, but the seal of the Spider which he sought was not revealed. Then this man was not the Devil himself! He glanced at his watch again, judged that enough time had elapsed, and asked a question of the white-faced recumbent lawyer whose chest rose and fell as in deep sleep.

"Who is the Devil?" he asked.

Silence for a while in the room, then Howard spoke clearly. "Peter Isong."

"What is his real name?"

"Peter Isong."

It seemed a dead man was talking so white and ghastly did Howard lie there, moving pale lips. He was in the grip of sodium-amytol, the truth drug. He could not answer untruthfully while he lay in this condition, but he could not talk long. Wentworth hurried.

"Where is the cavern?"

"I don't know."

"Where is Ann Beach?"

"In the cavern."

Wentworth sucked in a quick breath. Everything pointed back to that cavern which he could not locate, although he knew he had been there. Maddening to know that information was in his brain and wouldn't come out!

"What city is to be attacked next?" he hurried on.

"Albany," came the clear, toneless voice. Wentworth stiffened where he crouched. This city was to fall prey to the hell-blast of the Devil! But he must hurry. There had been an impediment to that last answer. The effect of the drug was fading.

"When?" he demanded tensely. "When will they attack Albany?"

"Tonight."

God! Wentworth's eyes grew wide as that shocking bit of information sank home.

"Will the governor be harmed?"

The lips opened, shut, opened again. Howard tossed his head as if in anguish, and the ghost of a "Yes" came from his lips. Abruptly Wentworth tensed forward. There had come a sudden, ghastly change in the lawyer's face—an ugly, bluish tint that spread rapidly from the nose outward across pallid cheeks. There came a convulsive jerking, a stiffening of the facial muscles. Delancey Howard would talk no more—now or ever! His heart, undoubtedly weak, had stopped beating....

Slowly Wentworth came to his feet, shook his head. A criminal had paid for his crimes with his life. But the Spider must hurry!

He sprang up, crossed toward the room where Nita had used the phone, the cane helping his left leg. His eyes were hard beneath the black silk mask, and his right fist was knotted at his side. He caught up the instrument and rapidly put through a long distance phone call to Stanley Kirkpatrick, his friend, the commissioner of New York police. Here they might scoff at him, the governor might deride his theories, but Kirkpatrick would accept his words without quibbling.

"Kirk," Wentworth spilled out, his words rapidly, "Albany is to be attacked tonight by the Bomb Men. I'm calling you because so far I've been unable to make these people up here believe what I report."

"What time, Dick?" came Kirkpatrick's crisp, decisive voice.

"I couldn't find that out," Wentworth went on.

"Rush troops here as fast as you can. Any excuse will do. Tell them the governor isn't able to communicate. He's threatened, I know.

"And listen, if you haven't heard this radio man, J. Osborne Pierce, listen in. He ought to be put off the air because of the terrorism his talks create. Arrest him.

"Another thing. Have a tracer put on Peter Isong—I-s-o-n-g—and find out all you can about him. That's the name the leader uses, and…."

The phone went dead in his hands and a shuddering blast beat against the windows. The attack was on!

CHAPTER 14
TO SAVE THE GOVERNOR

USING THE cane as a vaulting pole to bolster his bad leg, Wentworth crossed the room in long bounds, jerked open the door and was gone.

No need to use furtive escape now, no need to dodge police, for the blast that ripped down the telephone lines was repeated even as he raced down the hall. He knew that would be the police stations going up in dust. It was the way the gang worked.

As he skipped down the stairs that circled the elevator shaft, the lights went out and another blast shook the air.

They were making a thorough job of crippling the defenses of Albany before the looting. Wentworth hit the street, ludicrous with his hobbling speed. He hopped to his car. And now in the wake of those blasts, there was a vast weighty silence. Not a light gleamed anywhere. There was no movement.

Wentworth swung in a tire-moaning circle and headed for the offices of the governor. The papers had revealed he would be there late tonight and from him alone could more help come now. If he were killed—Wentworth knew the lieutenant governor. He was a man easily susceptible to hypnotism. It was clearly apparent in the wide credulous eyes and weak, small mouth. He would be subject to the mastery of the drugs and hypnotic eyes of the Devil. God knew, if Nita had fallen subject to that domination, then the lieutenant governor....

Wentworth crushed down the thought of Nita. It hurt. He slammed into the east side of the Capitol square, going north fast, pivoted around the northern side of the block and jerked to a halt before the broad steps of the building. Two men in uniform challenged him, guns and dazzling flashlights in hand.

Wentworth ran to meet them, shouting the name of Chief Reed of the city police. The men refused to give way, bracing themselves for the shock of Wentworth's awkward cane-vaulting rush.

When he had almost reached them, Wentworth ducked to one side and went behind them. Swiftly he struck with the butt of his gun and laid them unconscious on the steps. It was hard, but there was no other way. The governor must be saved. Even as he rushed now up these steps, it might be too late. The fuse that would fulminate the death charge and send the Capitol up in dust might already be lighted!

Wentworth rushed through the doors, down the long corridors. Another guard hastened to meet him at the door of the executive offices where lights glowed dimly.

"A bomb!" Wentworth yelled. "Bomb under building!"

The man stood firm, glowering uncertainly, and Wentworth plunged right up to him. He gestured with his right hand, the gun in his pocket now, and jolted the head of his cane upward to the man's chin with his left. The fellow reeled backward, the glass panel smashed and the door shuddered inward.

Wentworth hopped over his body, rushed toward an unlabeled door of ground glass. A vague shadow-form showed against it, in silhouette, even as Wentworth moved swiftly forward. The door opened and the governor thrust out his bald head, a gun in his fist. Behind him crowded two other men. A dozen flickering candles was their only light.

"A bomb!" Wentworth shouted. "There's one under this building. Come on Governor, get out fast!"

"Don't go," a man behind him cried. "It's a trap!" They jabbed excited fingers at the police guard prostrate in the shadows by the outer door.

Wentworth turned his head to stare back where they pointed, but kept moving toward the governor.

"Halt!" the governor got out swiftly, and his voice was almost in Wentworth's ear. Wentworth jerked his head about and seized the man's wrist in the same moment, twisting the gun loose. He jabbed its muzzle into the governor's ribs, jerked out his own to cover the two men behind him.

"Get out of here fast!" he ordered. "I tell you the building is going up in dust any moment."

He caught the governor in the small of the back with the gun and sent him reeling toward the door.

He kept on talking rapidly. "I hate to do this, but there's no other way." He jerked a glance over his shoulder at the others. "Pick up that policeman and bring him along," he ordered. "It's death to stay here."

AT A run, Wentworth lurching along awkwardly, they headed through the darkness for the front door. They blundered out. The moon threw dim light over the white and black asphalt street. The two guards Wentworth had felled there were staggering to their feet.

"Scatter!" Wentworth shouted. "This building is going to blow up!"

The two men stared and saw others in panic. They ran. Wentworth shoved the governor into his car, sprang behind the wheel and sent the machine in a skidding arc into the park, down through the stark, blast-torn trees. They skimmed around the black crater made by the bomb that had killed Senator Beach and suddenly, without warning, the top was ripped off the car.

A vast rush of burning air whipped past them. Wentworth felt his senses reeling and grabbed the emergency. The car wrenched violently and spun like a crazy top down State Street, came to a final jouncing halt with locked brakes skidding. Wentworth fought back the darkness from his reeling mind, turned heavily toward the governor beside him. The governor was staring back over his shoulder.

Wentworth twisted about, too. Where the State building had stood the moonlight threw black shadows into a crater. The Capitol had gone up in dust!

Wentworth said heavily, "Governor, I am the crank who warned you some days ago about the park bill. This is part of the same plot. Will you believe me now and turn every police force in the state on the problem of solving the crimes, turn out the militia to guard the towns that haven't been attacked?"

The governor's face was pale as death. His mouth was working so that the dim flashlight cast weird shadows over it.

"I will," he said. "God help me for a blind fool!"

Wentworth said grimly, "You can make what amends are possible by swift action. Call out the police and the national guard."

"I'll do that," the governor declared. He stared hard at his savior. "Who are you?"

Wentworth laughed, his voice hard. "I am the man the police call the most notorious criminal in the world. I am the Spider!"

Wentworth started the car with a lurch, as into the street from the next corner whirled a shouting, scattered mob of roughly clad men like a great black beast in the moonlight. They were cheering hoarsely, and over their heads they waved clubs—the looters!

Wentworth spun the wheel and whirled the car back up State

Street. Another looting mob was packed from house to house behind them, too! Could the car plow through them? Small chance. That mob would recognize the well-known bald head and the grim face of the governor and strike him down even if the auto crashed through. And the governor must be saved.

Wentworth spun the wheel again, headed for the nearby buildings. He rammed in a door, turned to the governor.

"Get out," he snapped. "Go through this building and out into the next street and escape."

Staring at Wentworth, the governor climbed out. "And you?" he questioned.

Wentworth threw back his head. Never had the flat mocking laughter of the Spider seemed so mad, never so horrible.

"There is work for the Spider!" he cried. He yanked the car backward, turned its nose and sent it hurtling toward the nearest mob!

CHAPTER 15
THE BATTLE FOR ALBANY

THE MOB jamming the street ahead was over a thousand strong. A dozen leaders ran in front urging the men on with wildly flung arms. Behind them, the mass thickened until they were packed shoulder to shoulder and ten to twenty men deep. Behind them other stragglers shouted and hurled curses into the air. It was a mad mob, filled with the mania of destruction, infuriated against all civilized authority by the skillful goading of the Devil's agitators.

Wentworth charged them at top speed. He steered directly at the midmost leader. The man threw up a revolver. Wentworth saw the glint from his headlights and ducked behind the protection of the car's cowling. Fragments of glass rained down upon him, fine as dust from the shatter-proof windshield.

Wentworth hurtled on, crouching far down behind the wheel. He caught a brief glimpse of the man jumping aside, then he wrenched the car violently about and ripped at full speed across the foremost rank of the mob. A man, struck by the right mudguard, hurtled like a bowling ball against the mob. A half dozen men spilled. Another tried to spring entirely across the car's front and, smacked by the radiator, catapulted twenty feet and smashed against a brick building.

Wentworth spun the wheel and ground down on the brakes. The car whined into a skidding turn, skated almost completely around. He yanked the throttle, twisted the steering gear and once more was juggernauting back across the front ranks of the mob, headed back across the hundred-foot breadth of State street. Leaders fired at him, but their aim was taken in frantic haste, and though lead clunked into the car, none hit the Spider who, narrow-eyed and with mouth grimly smiling, coolly went about the task of breaking up the marching men.

The second mob running from the opposite direction was closing in on him now, scarcely seventy-five feet away. Cobbles torn from the street whizzed through the air. A spattering gun fire struck chiefly among the mob Wentworth fought, and men fell screaming beneath the wheels of his car.

The mob began to turn back upon itself. Those in the front

ranks fought savagely with fists and clubs to flee from the bloodied ram of the car's nose. At the far side of the street, Wentworth whirled again with a wrench and a shriek of brakes, slammed two men down with the swinging rear and ploughed back again. He gouged more deeply into the mob's ranks this time, hurling men aside like broken dolls. Before he was half across the street, the last of the pack whirled and ran, streaming out over the park toward the cavity where the Capitol had stood.

Wentworth did not pursue. He spun the valiant car and charged head-on for the second mob. Once more the beat and hammer of bullets ripped the car. Its radiator was spouting steam and boiling water from a dozen lead-gouged holes. The headlights were smashed. One tire had gone flat and Wentworth was forced to throw his entire weight on the wheel to hold the auto to its course. But still no bullets struck vital spots in the machinery, none reached Wentworth.

Scrambling men battled to clear a way for him, splitting the ranks down the middle. Once more he slewed the car about and a man screamed as the bucking rear battered about. Wentworth coursed across the front rank. The car chattered and pounded, its engine laboring against a drained and steaming radiator. Grimly Wentworth drove on, speed cut nearly in half, and smashed into the foremost rank.

BUT THIS mob had seen the havoc wrought upon the other. Even above their own sullen shouting came the screams of the injured. The street was spotted with their broken bodies. The new pack had no stomach for battle, but turned and fled before

111

Wentworth could whirl at the end of his shattering charge to cut back across their path again.

A single man stood his ground. Wentworth drove directly at him, snatching out his gun. This was one of the leaders, he knew, one of those who had been inciting the mobs to riot and loot. He above all others was guilty, and apparently he was determined to strike down this obstacle to the Devil's plans.

The pounding engine pulled the car about, and the dimming ray from its single headlight swept over the man. Wentworth had his pistol leveled—but he lowered it without firing. His mouth shut in a grim line. The man held a child as a shield before him, a little girl who kicked and squirmed but was helpless in the grip of the man's left arm. And over the girl's shoulder the defiant Devil's leader leveled a gun!

He drove directly at the man.

The leader stood firm as Wentworth bored down on him, stood firm until the car was within twenty feet of him. Then he hurled the child squarely in the path of the car and sprang back lightly, ready with his gun. The child was between Wentworth and the gunman. Thoughts were a lightning flash of speed in Wentworth's mind. He knew the trap instantly. The man hoped that he would swerve and either wreck the car or lose control. In either case, the man would be able to shoot him down while he was too occupied with the car to defend himself.

The entire state was at stake in this second. No doubt of that. No one save himself could defeat this gigantic menace which was ravishing cities, destroying thousands of lives, millions of dollars of property. He could save himself for the battle and probably kill the leader, too, if he would drive his crushing wheels over the child's body....

These things he realized in the instant that he saw the man hurl the child to the ground. Before the girl had landed on the pavement, had raised her voice in a feeble, hopeless scream, Wentworth had made his choice. He seized the steering wheel high up on the left and wrenched.

The car swung about, rear wheels shrieking on the pavement. It heeled over on two tires, slanting hazardously. Wentworth jerked his head about. Even if the car crashed completely over, he saw that the child would be safe. She was a black, writhing shadow on the cobbles. Yes, the child was safe, but Wentworth....

WHILE THE car teetered, almost motionless as momentum and gravity fought the battle to determine whether it should crash on its side or bounce back on its slashed tires, the leader darted forward so that he could make sure of a shot that would kill Wentworth.

The Spider was helpless, fighting the car with pumping throttle, with his body's weight and the wrenching wheel. He had been compelled to drop his gun for that swift maneuver and it lay upon the floor.

Abruptly, Wentworth abandoned the fight with the wheel. He knew that meant the car would crash over on its side, probably would hurl him clear into the street almost at the feet of the gunman. He flung himself toward the gun on the floor. The car lurched, tilted higher. The extra weight jerked it over and with an almost stately slowness, it flopped on its side.

The impact rolled Wentworth clear, tumbling across the

pavement. The leader danced backward out of the way, his gun a glinting arc in the moonlit street.

As he rolled, Wentworth fired two, three, four times, snapping the bullets wildly into the air. He knew he stood small chance of scoring a hit, but hoped to disconcert the gunman so that the other's lead would fly wide, too.

Bullets smacked the pavement about him, but when the force of his fall had expended itself, he was still un-hit. He flung himself up on one stiff arm and snapped his fifth and final shot with lightning speed.

The man's gun spat once more. But the powder flame stabbed straight down at the pavement. As Wentworth, dodging, hauled himself painfully to his feet, he saw the leader sway, stagger a pace forward and pitch down on his face.

Wentworth turned heavily and walked toward the little girl, who lay sobbing on the pavement waiting for death. He bent slowly, touched her black hair.

"It's all right, child," he said gently. "Run home now."

The girl jerked up from the pavement, stared up through the dimness of the moonlight and saw only that a man stood over her.

"It's all right," said Wentworth again. "That man won't bother you any more."

The child struggled to her feet, still staring. She whirled abruptly and ran away as fast as she could, screaming for her mother. Wentworth shook his head, pressing a massaging palm to his brow, then he lifted his eyes firmly and swept the street with a swiftly appraising glance.

The last of the mob had fled into side streets and the main avenue except for the bodies of the dead and the screaming injured, was empty. He limped toward the protecting shadows of nearby buildings, but stopped abruptly as a man darted from a drug store and raced off, with one swiftly fearful backward glance.

Others poured from the structure, and with a slamming dazzling blast whose concussion pinned Wentworth against the wall and batted the other men down like a cannon ball, the store split into fragments and soared into the air.

But there was no rain of debris. There was nothing but a fine choking dust in the air. The drug store had been literally blown up in nothingness!

Wentworth thrust himself out from the building and went on heavy feet toward the man who had fled the store. That one heaved to his feet and ran on. He had thrown himself down and escaped the main impact. He pivoted a corner, slapped his feet down under the squatty shade trees of deserted Hamilton street. A full block he ran through black moon shadow and pale light, then, slowing, turned another corner toward State Street. **DOGGEDLY WENTWORTH** clung to his heels. The violence of action had made him forget for a while his wounded leg and he had overtaxed its weakened muscles. Now the reaction had set in and once more the aching fever throb was in his blood. But he pushed on doggedly and, turning a corner, saw the man join a group outside a massive bank at the corner of Main street. A street car was stalled half around the curve without a single person in it. Its windows were smashed. An automobile had been swept against a store front by panic or explosion and had smashed a plate glass window.

As Wentworth watched, the men moved in a compact mass toward the bank, and from its metal doors a machine gun stammered. Two attackers went down, the rest sprang behind the stalled street car. One drew back his arm and flung it forward as if throwing something. The steel bank doors vanished in a puff and flash that left the entrance black and shattered like a crazy man's lop-sided mouth.

The attackers charged that door, and now no machine gun stuttered in its defense. Wentworth stepped behind a steel lamp post and deliberately fired into the ranks from behind. He shot first the one who had hurled the bomb. The attack split, and the five remaining men broke for cover. Wentworth dropped two before they found protection, two behind the wrecked car, another behind the buttressed steps of the bank.

Wentworth drew himself up stiffly behind the pole, and it clanged like a fire gong to the clapper-beat of the return fire. He reeled and dropped in the gutter, covered by the granite curb, and the men broke for the door of the bank again. Three times Wentworth fired in slow sequence, and at each crack of his automatic another man fell. The last one lay with his head in the darkness of the bank's interior.

Wentworth looked swiftly over the moon-silvered street. It was entirely deserted. Up toward the Capital, fully a score of bodies lay in the street, the shattered remnants of the mob. The Laurelton Hotel, where Wentworth first had stayed, where Nita and Ram Singh were quartered now, was a half block up the street from the bank. Wentworth's lips lost their fighting smile. The corners turned down bitterly. Perhaps in Nita's quarters, he might find some clue to the whereabouts of the leader or the cavern. They would be sure to provide *her* with protection after she had betrayed the Spider for them. The thought of her was pain, and deliberately Wentworth tortured himself with her treachery.

With a slow, dragging step that was ominous in its heaviness, he crossed the street. The hotel entrance was barricaded, but he persuaded the bright-faced clerk to let him in and made his portentous way up darkened stairways to the door of Nita's quarters. He listened tensely. Within was no sound. He lifted his hand to knock, then paused. His face was without expression, his eyes stony. He rapped three times sharply.

Inside the silence remained unbroken. He raised his hand again, and the door was snatched away from beneath his knuckles and a gun menaced him, a gun in the firm dark hand of Ram Singh. From behind the Hindu came the glare of a hand torch. For a moment, Ram Singh did not recognize him, then seeing his eyes and their intent regard, he thrust the pistol into his wide white sash and salaamed almost to the floor.

"*Sahib!*" he choked.

Wentworth slugged him with his automatic and knocked him unconscious back through the doorway!

CHAPTER 16
THE SPIDER
AND THE TRAITOR

"**D**ICK!" GASPED a voice Wentworth knew, the voice of Nita.

His face did not change, but he held the gun ready in his hand. Fever worked in his brain, the gnawing of a week of pain, the terrific exertions that would have tried the stamina of a man in perfect health, which were as the labors of Hercules to the weakened Wentworth. His dry, bright eyes sought Nita behind the light.

"Bring out your allies and kill me!" he rasped.

"Dick!" Nita cried again. The light came toward him slowly, but it was not pointed at his eyes now, and he could see the pale loom of Nita's night-robe behind it.

"So, they've deserted you!" he bit out. "You see, Nita, it does not pay to turn on old friends. They are more trustworthy than your new."

He went forward woodenly, limping heavily, and took the flashlight from Nita's hand. He shut the door behind him and snapped the bolt, then made a thorough search of the entire suite of rooms and found nothing. He came back and turned the dazzle of the beam on Nita's face. It was drawn and pale, the blue eyes large. Her night-robe was orchid silk, and the sash about her waist was velvet and yellow. Never, Wentworth thought, had he seen her so beautiful. His lips writhed in a futile attempt to smile.

"Dick," said Nita anxiously, "what's the matter, dear?"

Wentworth looked at her without reply, his eyes cold.

"Surely, Dick, you don't believe, you couldn't...."

"Believe!" Wentworth snorted a single bark of laughter. *"I know!"*

He laughed again, and in his throat it turned into a sob. He choked it down, opened his mouth to speak and felt the knot of that sob still in his throat. He clamped his teeth together. Was this the Spider, who choked with womanish tears in his throat?

Wentworth's hands were aching with the tension of their clenching fingers, his forearms were cramped by the strain. Something swelled in his chest—and that hellish pain gnawed like a live thing at his thigh. He shook his head violently. This was no time for weakness.

He had saved the governor from the Devil's plot; he had saved one bank from looters. Soldiers must be on the way by plane now from nearby points, summoned by Kirkpatrick. These things were well enough, but the Devil still roamed the earth with his disintegrating blasts, leading the mobs of pillagers to kill and maim and destroy. And Nita knew the answer.

Nita? It was no longer Nita who stood before him. This was merely a nameless woman who held facts he must know.

He took a slow step forward. "Tell me what you know about the Devil and his plot," he commanded harshly.

NITA WAS staring at him with those blue eyes of hers wide and hurt. She said, "Of course, Dick. That lawyer you asked me to get information from, Delancey Howard, told me that the explosive was made from some sort of horrible fish whose name he didn't know and that these fish were kept in some cavern in the parks. He didn't know which part of the parks, but thought the cavern was somewhere near Ausable Chasm."

A cavern with horrible fish... Something in the back of Wentworth's brain thrust forward for a moment, a memory of a vast cavern... Then it was gone. He struck his forehead with his fist, thinking, thinking. The memory could not be recaptured.

"You are telling the truth," he said in a strained voice. "I know that. Your friends at least kept no secrets from you. But they must have told you something further—how to find safety when the attack began on Albany. Where were you to go?"

"I didn't know Albany was to be attacked!" It was a cry. "Oh, Dick, what is the matter with you?"

Nita moved a timid step forward, her white hands outstretched in pleading.

"Poor Dick," she said softly. "You limp. You have been wounded." His hands clenched his head and the reddish wig became displaced and his patch bandage there became visible. "Dick! Your head is hurt, too! Here, let me—"

Her hands were reaching for his corded wrists. They snapped sharply down, and Nita fell back with a small cry in her throat at the stark hatred of his eyes. She crushed a hand against her lips.

"I remember now!" he cried. "Howard told you that if any trouble came you were to go to his apartment. Howard's home is the rallying place." He took a furious step toward her. "You were protecting your new friends, eh? Telling what you had to, fooling me, tricking me like you did at Howard's home, calling police and firing at me!"

"You're mad, Dick!"

Wentworth swept an arm violently across his body, knocking aside the pleading in her voice. "I'm crazy, surely. Crazy ever to trust you. I won't again."

He started toward the door on quick feet, whirled and came back. "I forgot. I mustn't leave you to warn them I'm coming," he whispered.

He limped past her to the bathroom, came back with adhesive tape. "Turn around and cross your wrists!" he ordered her sternly.

Nita stared at him. There was a big tear on each cheek and dry sobbing tugged at her lips. Her arms hung limply at her side. "No, Dick," she begged. "No. Dick, you're out of your head. Stay here with me, dear."

"For your friends to trap?" The sob was gone from his throat now. His voice was sneering. "Turn around and cross your wrists!"

Nita still looked at him with tear-blurred, pleading eyes. She shook her head slowly, not in refusal, but in despair.

Wentworth's lips writhed. "Will you compel me to use force?"

The sobs welled up in Nita's throat now and shook her shoulders terribly. Her head drooped. She turned and crossed her wrists. Wentworth strapped them roughly with the tape. Across the sweet red lips he had kissed he crossed two strips as a gag. He pushed her to a davenport and bound her ankles.

The taxi ran wild, swerved and dived into the woods.

Nita's eyes were no longer wet. They were hot blue flames of anger, but she made no protest, no resistance.

When he had secured her, Wentworth bound Ram Singh,

slammed the door and went down the hall violently toward the fire escape steps. His wounded leg was dragging so that it would scarcely sustain his weight. His left hand gripped it. His face was set as ice, his mouth a straight, savage slit. But as he walked, his pace slowed. He reached the fire door and abruptly his shoulders contorted convulsively.

He caught the doorjamb with his hands and threw back his head. And dry, horrible sobs racked his body. No tears came to his eyes. They stared straight up at the black ceiling above him, and the shuddering wrenches of his grief continued to beat upon his heart and brain. In his mind was only one word. "Nita. Nita! *Nita!*"

SLOWLY THE agony of his sorrow left him. He was weak and shaken, but he did not even glance down the blackness of the hall toward the room where those two lay bound. He opened the fire door and went heavily down the stairs.

Over the dark streets the drone of airplane motors brought the promise of relief to the city. Those would be the advance guard of the troops Kirkpatrick was sending. Distantly the overwhelming blast of one of the disintegrator bombs let go and glass in the door at his side shuddered. He felt the beat of the air upon his face. He moved up the street, bracing his left arm against the buildings he passed. He stepped over a dead man crushed as if by a steam roller....

At long last he found a taxi parked at the curb with its engine running, the driver dead at the wheel with a bullet through his head. A stray shot.... Wentworth tumbled the body to the street, slid behind the wheel and awkwardly using his right foot on the clutch pedal got the car into motion. He yanked the throttle wide and whizzed through streets where the only living things were skulking looters. He heard a woman screaming. It was a spurt of sound drowned instantly in the all-enveloping fury of the engine.

He whammed into Lake Drive on two wheels, righted the taxi with a quick wrench and a kick at the brake pedal and shot on once more. Howard's apartment was the rallying spot. There he would find the assembled leaders of the Devil's army of hell.

He yanked on the emergency, and the rear wheels slewed around and smacked the curb, bounced out again and stopped.

He dragged across the pavement and through the dark hallway of the apartment house, fought his way slowly up the stairs to the fifth floor and moved, soundlessly except for the scrape at his almost helpless leg, to the door of Howard's apartment. It was open, and Wentworth pushed in, listening. No sound there, no sign of life. He spattered the beam of his torch over the place with a single short flash. No one here, no one except the corpse of Delancey Howard on the floor.

Wentworth cut off the light, made his way to the davenport against the wall and dropped upon it. He sat stiffly, waiting.

His grief had left an emptiness within him, a drained vacant feeling. Nothing remained now except his task.

It was an hour later, an hour during which Wentworth did not move, that there came a slight scratching at the door. He pushed up and crossed the room. His leg had grown stiff, but the rest had helped it. He grasped the knob, clenched his ready gun, and yanked open the door.

Someone cried out and stumbled into the room against him in the darkness. Wentworth thrust the man off with the muzzle of his gun and squeezed light from his hand torch. The man was a square-shouldered fellow with a heavy, wide jaw, ears close against his head. He grinned, crinkling his eye corners.

"Jackson!" said Wentworth in a dead voice, "Have you sold out, too?"

CHAPTER 17
AMBUSH OF THE CAVERN

THE SMILE faded slowly from Jacksons wide, good-natured face. "I know where that gang is, sir," he reported stiffly. "If the major will come with me—"

The lapse into familiar language steadied Wentworth somewhat, but his eyes still burned with fever madness. He still held the gun on his chauffeur.

"Take your gun out, Jackson, and hold it by the barrel," His voice was cold. Jackson obeyed without an instant's hesitation. "Hand it to me." Jackson did that, too. "Take me to the gang," he ordered then, and Jackson executed right about smartly and marched off down the hall, Wentworth dragging his pain behind him.

Outside the apartment they entered the taxi Wentworth had appropriated and Jackson drove while his master sat beside him with an automatic in his hand.

"Lucky, finding you this way, sir," said Jackson. "The troops are taking over the town, but we can still get through if we move fast. It's out near Ausable Chasm."

Wentworth stared straight ahead, gun ready.

"I couldn't find you at the Stagler Hotel," Jackson went on cheerfully. "So I hunted up Miss Nita and found her all tied up. She said you had come over to Howard's place, so I came too."

Wentworth asked coldly, "You untied her?"

"Of course, sir."

"Then we will probably be ambushed on the way to Ausable Chasm," said Wentworth in the same dead tones. "I warn you that if you attempt to slow when they spring the trap you and she have laid for me, I will shoot you dead. Understand, Jackson?"

Jackson threw a side glance at his employer, the muscles knotting and twisting beneath the taut brown skin over his jaw bones.

"Understand, Jackson?"

Jackson swallowed hard. "Yes, Major."

Wentworth nodded slowly once, and did not again take his eyes off the white road. Miles slid backward beneath the whirring tires. The drone of the motor was a continuous, deep song. Slowly the trees at the roadside took form with the gray of first dawn behind them. That passed, and rosy light touched the road.

"Five miles to Ausable Chasm, sir," said Jackson. "The gang has its headquarters a mile this side and off to the left of the road. It's in a cavern."

Wentworth nodded once more slowly. "The ambush is long in materializing," he said. "It cannot be delayed much longer." He tested the safeties on the two automatics he had, one in his hand, one in his lap. The car droned on, swooped downgrade toward a stone culvert. Then, without warning, a machine gun chattered from the roadside.

Jackson lurched sideways in his seat and the taxi ran wild, swerved once, and again, and dived into the woods on the opposite side of the highway. Two small pines growing close together stopped it. The taxi slid its front axle up their rough bark, lifting with their springing thrust, then stopped. The trees snapped.

Wentworth heaved out behind the car. He leveled his automatic at Jackson's head. "I warned you," he said.

Jackson did not answer. There was a smear of blood across his forehead. He was unconscious, or dead. Wentworth lowered his gun, heard the hammer of bullets drumming on the body of the taxi. He crept away from it into the thick shelter of the trees.

WENTWORTH'S FACE was like that of a corpse. The flesh was yellowish, as if drained of living blood. His eyes were dry and bright.

On into the woods he forced his way, moving silently as an Indian, working nearer and nearer to the road's edge. He peered through thinning leaves and in the shrubbery across the highway, caught a slight movement, spotted the glint of metal. His lips twitched stiffly, but there was no grim smile as was the Spider's wont when he went into battle. He raised the Luger he had taken from Jackson and squeezed the trigger once.

Above the thin crack of the pistol, he heard the dying scream of a man. Wentworth pushed through the shrubbery and ducked into the open, moved with his slow limp across the road. He shoved into the underbrush and looked down at the body on the ground, the face glimmering in the early gray light.

Impassively, he drew his cigarette lighter, stooped, and pressed its base to the forehead of the dead man. When he had lifted it, a spot glowed red as blood there. His Spider's seal was like a sinister, leering eye.

Suddenly Wentworth threw back his head and laughed wildly. He shouted a formless sound into the soft morning.

"Death!" he howled. "Death to the Devil!"

For a moment after that mad cry had been hurled through the woods, there was absolute silence. Even the birds ceased their paean to the day. Then distantly there came a halloo. Wentworth's lips moved now, moved in a ferocious smile. He picked up the machine gun, picked up an extra hundred-round drum and looped it over his shoulder with his belt for a sling. His automatics he thrust into his belt. Heavily burdened, moving more slowly than ever, he wove through the woods.

Where was that man who had hallooed dimly? Over here somewhere to the left of the road was the cavern headquarters of the gang, Jackson had said. Had Jackson lied? Had he merely led him into an ambush? Wentworth paused and dragged the sleeve of his coat across his forehead and mouth. The fake mustache came loose, too. Most of the makeup had been sweated off, and the grim, lean lines of Wentworth's own pain-twisted face showed through.

He halted and stripped off his coat, slung the ammunition drum back on his shoulder, shifted the automatics, pushed on. He burned with a consuming desire for only one thing now, death for these fiends who had looted and slaughtered, who had stripped him of everything he held dear in life—everything save honor and his fierce determination to kill, kill, kill until the last man had paid the price of his infamy.

A GENTLE slope lay ahead of Wentworth. There, through the trees, he could see the ground rise sharply from a small brook, rise until it towered mountainously above him. His eyes took cognizance of that, his mind automatically began to plan for the reconnaissance before the advance—and something moved by the brook!

A man stood and shouted, "Hey, Summers!"

Wentworth used his Colt, and the crack of the gun was like the thunderbolt of a god of old. The man took the lead in his chest, threw up his hands and pitched backward into the ravine through which the brook trickled, The echo of the shot clapped back from the mountain ahead, and after it came shouts and the crash of men charging down grade.

Wentworth drove down the hill. He reached the ravine and dropped into it while the shooting was still a hundred yards away.

He grinned down at the corpse beside which he stood, then stooped and branded his forehead with the seal. He caught the man's shoulders and heaved upward, tossed the body to the rim of the ravine, its face toward the charging men. A pistol cracked from the wood and the corpse jerked with an unpleasant wheezing sound in its throat as the bullet smacked into its chest. Wentworth fired coolly. The new gunman did not cry out. He slapped down on his face in the earth mold at the foot of the grade. The crashing behind him stopped.

Steadily Wentworth waited. It was five minutes before movement betrayed the first of his new attackers, and Wentworth burned him down. The second tried to flee, and Wentworth's bullet drilled through his skull from behind. Then he climbed laboriously out of the ditch, and, twice more affixing the seal, went on up the hill. A mound of yellow mud that seemed vaguely familiar loomed before him, dumped in the middle of the green forest. He shook his head.

If the memory that was at the back of his brain would only come clear, he would know what this was all about.

Heavily, with an intolerable weight seeming to press upon his head and chest. Wentworth circled the heap of yellow mud and discovered a low opening into the face of the hill. He scarcely glanced at it a second time, but drove his flagging body on. For an instant he paused at the tunnel's lips, then, grim and silent, he crouched and shuffled into the darkness.

It was Stygian, that darkness, unrelieved by any faintest ray of light. For ten feet the shadow of the sun penetrated, and after that was only thick, choking blackness. There was a chill in the air and a damp, earthy smell. Wentworth did not use his hand torch. He pushed on with the whispering, hissing echo of his dragging feet the only sound in his ears.

Something in his mind was clicking now. The cavern air seemed fresher and he knew that this tunnel ran straight ahead and that there was no immediate danger in his path. Perhaps it was this same unconscious memory that made him pause presently, and send a single questing ray out into the black curtain before him to hurl the darkness back for a brief instant and reveal the shimmering ebony waters of a lake—the lake of ugly, unseen peril, where man-killing eels lurked!

But if his memory had served him before, it failed now. Slowly he began to divest himself of his clothing to swim that fatal lake!

When he had stripped to his shorts, Wentworth arranged machine gun and ammunition drum and pistols in a tight bundle bound with his shirt and tied them to the top of his head with the sleeves knotted beneath his chin. Then he moved heavily toward the black, lapping edge of the lake where swam the man-killing electric eels! The air was heavy with their musk....

CHAPTER 18
THREE MEN DIE

ON THE point of plunging into those lethal waters, Wentworth paused and jerked up his head. He switched out the light. From behind him came the stealthy whisper of feet.

Wentworth withdrew his feet quietly from the water where the red eyes of the eels still swarmed and crept to the side of the passageway where he stood—beside the tunnel mouth. Water lapped his insteps. The whisper of feet was louder now. Could the man possibly think he was moving silently? Wentworth eased his burden of weapons to a pinnacle stalagmite and slipped out an automatic. He reversed it, frowning. He was in no condition for a hand-to-hand fight. Even at the cost of bringing the entire gang down upon him, he might be forced to shoot.

The footsteps were quite near now, and Wentworth tensed himself, ready to hop forward on his one good leg and strike. The feet crunched on gravel and Wentworth raised his gun.

"Major!" a man whispered. "It's Jackson, sir."

Wentworth fanned flashlight glare into the tunnel mouth and Jackson whirled to face him. The bullet rip was bloody across his forehead and his face was drained of all color. He jerked up his hands.

"Major?" he questioned.

"Yes," said Wentworth tersely. "There's a lake. We'll have to strip and swim for it, Jackson." He was watching the man closely.

Jackson said, "Yes, Major," and immediately began to take off tunic and trousers. In a few moments, he was ready and advanced to the edge of the water. "You'd better wait here, sir, and let me find out how far the other shore is. You can guide me back with the light if I can't find any other exit."

"It's better together," Wentworth said, and switched off the light. Once more, Jackson at his side, he started for the deadly water.

"Shhh!" he warned abruptly. "Listen."

From the darkness came a distant sound of wood rubbing against wood. It was more vibration than actual sound.

"What is it, sir?"

"Paddle hitting boat," Wentworth told him succinctly.

Suspicion of Jackson still pecked at his brain. In the darkness, he edged away from him. "You take one side of the tunnel and I'll take the other," he said. "When I flash the light on him, you take him. My leg makes maneuvering rather difficult."

"Yes, sir," Jackson replied calmly. "That would be better. I found some men dead in the woods with the seal of the Spider on their foreheads and took a couple of guns and some extra ammunition from their bodies."

"Don't shoot unless you have to," Wentworth warned, and the two fell silent waiting while the jar of wood on wood came nearer and nearer and the drip of water joined the sound. A small glow showed in the darkness and soon it was possible to make out the outlines of a man in a canoe which carried a small lantern in its bottom. The man must steer by compass, Wentworth thought, then he saw that two other men were behind the one that wielded the paddle.

The men were at the mercy of the machine gun, of course, but firing it would warn the other members of the gang. Still, if the three landed, they might be difficult to overpower. Wentworth groped behind him and found a large rock fragment. He picked this up and poising it like a shot, heaved it up into the darkness.

It vanished at once, but in a split second of time, it whipped into view again, plunging downward into the glow of the lantern. It struck the edge of the canoe and the three men shouted in surprise and terrified unison. The paddler wrenched about to look behind him and the frail craft rocked violently. The men began to gabble at once, shouting orders to one another to sit still, but the damage was done. With a shrill concerted shriek of absolute terror, the three spilled into the water.

Darkness swooped down on the scene as the lantern was engulfed. But the darkness was filled with the thrashing of their fear, the lathering splash of the waters. And, suddenly, Wentworth was aware of moving points of light. They were like red sparks, but they traveled always in pairs, and they streaked toward one central point like water sucked down a drain—the spot where a moment ago the canoe had upset. The red sparks reached that spot and, as abruptly as the darkness had fallen, the shouts of the men ceased and the splashing ceased. For a moment longer, the echoes lived with their cries, then they, too, were stilled, and abysmal silence brooded over the place.

WENTWORTH, STARING into the darkness with bulging eyes, felt a pain sweep through his head like a fresh breeze, and suddenly he remembered! The death of these men and the death of some other men coincided. He knew what those red sparks were in the water and he leaned back against the angle of the rock wall, feeling faint at the thought that he had been on the point of plunging into those waters where the electric eels had just killed. Jackson had been ready to brave them... Then Jackson was loyal!

Wentworth thrust himself out from the wall and flung the blade of his light into the darkness. The water had begun already to lose its roiled and turbulent surface. Ripples were washing off into the blackness beyond and the canoe, upside down, bobbed gently on the infant swells.

"I'll get it, sir," Jackson volunteered.

"Don't go near that water!" Wentworth spat out the words like lightning. "Those sparks are the eyes of electric eels. They can knock you unconscious with a touch, and drowning follows."

Jackson, already one stride toward the black verge, stopped with a suddenness that made a tremor run over his broad-beamed, powerful body. "Good—*God!*" he whispered.

Of the men who had fallen overboard, there was not a sign. Wentworth drew from the packet still strapped beneath his arms, the tool kit of the Spider from which he never parted while on a crusade, a length of fine cord scarcely as large as a lead pencil. Swiftly, he knotted the end about a fragment of rock and tossed it over the capsized canoe.

Within seconds, he had the boat grating on the tiny beach. He restored the cord—it was silk that tested seven hundred pounds and police, when they found fragments of it, called the cord the Spider's web—to the packet and with Jackson's help righted the canoe.

Paddles were in reach and within two minutes, not bothering to clothe themselves again, but stuffing the garments into the canoe and loading the machine gun, they were steering straight out onto the black water.

"It is only necessary to go straight ahead," Wentworth said quietly. "There is a tunnel entrance straight ahead."

Jackson twisted where he knelt in the front of the canoe and stared back at Wentworth with a white face. "You knew—about the eels."

"Amnesia," said Wentworth briefly. "I had forgotten everything about this place except a hazy idea that it was somewhere. Now, I remember everything. When those three men died, I remembered. Straight ahead, Jackson."

"Yes, Major."

In total darkness then, the flash switched off, Wentworth stroked quietly out over the waters of the subterranean lake There was no sound of wood jarring against wood now, no drip of the paddles. They moved without a murmur. But the red sparks of death trailed them and Wentworth visualized the thick, loathsome bodies writhing beneath the surface, each one capable of inflicting a knockout blow to a man with a mere touch of its tail....

CHAPTER 19
IN HELL

WENTWORTH DROVE the canoe through the water until there was a small riffling liquid note from its slicing keel. He caught himself sharply, let the boat drift. He shielded the flashlight below the gunwales and thumbed the button. Gleaming facets cast back its light from a thousand overhead crystals, and directly ahead of them loomed the black mouth of the second tunnel. He had steered a true course.

He clicked off the light and let the canoe drift on until it grated with a small rasp upon the shelf. Then cautiously, the two men clambered over the thwarts to the shelf. At Wentworth's order, the canoe was secured by a strand of the "web" tied to a stalagmite and the craft itself was thrust out of sight in the darkness against the cavern wall.

Then, bristling with the guns thrust into the belts of their shorts, the only other clothing their shoes and ammunition clips, the two moved on along the tunnel, silently except that Wentworth's dragging leg rasped ever so slightly. Jackson carrying the machine gun, they went through a mile of tunnel, and the brief flash of Wentworth's torch revealed the square chamber and the crude throne chair where the Devil had trapped him, but there the passage seemed to end. There were oil flares along the walls and blankets on the floor indicated that the guards of the cavern had slept there.

In the red flickering flare of the torches that played luridly over their stripped bodies and glinted on the metal of their weapons, the two men stared at each other.

"What do you know about this place, Jackson?" Wentworth asked slowly.

Jackson shrugged. "I spent five days searching the Ausable Chasm road after the trail of creosote led to it, and on the fifth day, I saw a heavily loaded truck come very, very cautiously out of a wood road. The truck jounced once, and a man jumped off the seat and told the driver that if he did that again, they'd both go up in dust."

Wentworth's eyes gleamed. "And that road led from here?"

"From here, yes, sir."

"There must be another tunnel off the lake," Wentworth decided and slowly went back along the passageway, hauled in the canoe with its gossamer moorings. They began a slow tour of the lake shore, burning an old flare within the boat, leading with them a school of hungry, red-eyed eels.

The walls of the cavern were overhanging at some points; at others they sloped away through a forest of crystal columns where mocking shadows danced, but explorations on foot revealed nothing there until, when they had traveled what Wentworth estimated was two miles, they saw a regular line of floats on the surface of the water, small cork floats such as are used to support fish seines.

Instantly Wentworth extinguished the flare and, fingering

along the cork floats, tugged the canoe softly along. After five minutes of this, he detected a curve in the line of progress. Another three minutes and the cork line ended. They waited then in tense silence, listening, but hearing nothing risked a brief flash of light.

They were within ten feet of another such tunnel mouth as that they had left before, but this was fully fifty feet across and upon its floor was a windlass such as is used for hauling in nets. All about the place was a strong fish-oil odor that mingled strangely with the musk. Wentworth recalled with sharp excitement that Nita had said the explosive employed some substance taken from a horrible fish. He uttered a low exclamation.

"This is why they wanted the park lands, Jackson," he said swiftly. "These electric eels are what they use to make the explosive. They wanted to gain peaceful possession so they could manufacture the stuff quietly until they had plenty for their purpose. Then they could snap their fingers at the world.

"Once the fight was forced out into the open, they kept on working for the park lands to distract attention from their real activities. No one would think they were using them illegally when they were seeking peaceful possession. Oh, it's clever, damnably clever."

Jackson paddled quietly to the lip of the beach and once more they concealed the canoe far off to one side with the thin mooring line of silk. Then, stealthily as before, they stole up this wide tunnel.

A HUNDRED yards in, it began to narrow. It twisted and

turned as if it might have been the course of some ancient river and finally sounds came to Wentworth, sounds of something trundling over the earth.

Wentworth flung the light about them. The walls dripped steadily, but they were solid and offered no place of concealment. He could not fight it out with these demons yet. He did not know the secret of the explosive or where it was made. He spoke to Jackson and stole back to the lake's edge.

"Take the canoe," Wentworth ordered. "Go and lead the governor's troops here. I'll see to it that there is no one to prevent their entrance from the outside tunnel."

"But you, sir." Jackson stood squarely before him. "You have been wounded twice. Your leg must be feverish and you can scarcely walk on it. You are one man against God knows how many, and you have no means of escaping if I take the canoe. You haven't a chance in a thousand."

Wentworth's lips were grimly set. Slowly their corners twisted in a smile that the flickering oil flare made fantastic. His eyes were bitter. "You are lessening my chances by arguing," he said flatly. "As to my escape, when I have wiped out this nest of killers, that is my own affair. Go!"

Jackson opened his mouth to speak, but meeting Wentworth's iron gaze, he saluted, and when he had given Wentworth the machine gun, he pivoted on his heel and climbed into the canoe.

Wentworth smothered the torch and turned back into the cavern. As they had passed through it the last time, he had spotted a crevasse into which he thought he could just squeeze his body. Once the men had passed him, he could.... Here it was. He gripped its edges and dragged himself inward, still clinging to the machine gun and extra ammunition.

He wriggled and squirmed his way back into the slit between two planes of rock until the walls seemed a vise that wrung the last shreds of vigor from his tortured body. Still he was not out of sight. A side glance might detect him. The echoing voices of the approaching men and their tramping feet were loud now. The dancing beams of their lights glistened on the walls. Wentworth turned his head toward the opening, scarcely a foot away, and leveled a pistol.

The trooping feet were almost beside him and the first dazzle of a flaring oil torch almost blinded Wentworth as it went by. The men did not glance to right or left as they walked, but muttered one to the other. First a close group of four went by, then three more straggling individually followed by six more talking with animation. One man in every group carried an oil flare. Five more men straggled past, two more, then lights and voices began to recede. There were twenty men, and Wentworth recalled that the net was set. They were going to haul in that seine of eels. He would have time to penetrate further into the cavern.

Wentworth squeezed a few inches toward the tunnel, then froze in his tracks. Thudding feet were approaching rapidly. A man traveling alone and running fast flashed by. He had a miner's cap, a lamp on his cap visor blazing his path for him.

"Hey!" he shouted to the men ahead and his voice beat along the tunnel.

WENTWORTH HEARD the others halloo back and he

eased even closer to the lip, until a wrench would tear him free of the inpressing sides of the crevasse. If he guessed right, this last man was a messenger. He would be returning in a few minutes, more slowly than he had first traveled, but still alone....

Wentworth had five minutes to wait before the shifting shadows on the side walls and floor of the tunnel, like the shift on the surface of a road before an auto's headlights, heralded his return. Wentworth tensed, gun reversed in his hand.

Slowly the footsteps came on, plodding methodically now as contrasted with their earlier speed. Now a hundred feet away, now fifty, twenty-five—fifteen— Wentworth braced a hand to thrust himself clear—ten feet, five. Wentworth could see him now, slouching along, the beam from his cap light wavering across the floor.

Exactly opposite Wentworth's hiding place, the man halted and, drawn by one of those curious coincidences that some term mental telepathy, stared directly into Wentworth's eyes! The dazzling beam of his lamp followed his gaze. His mouth dropped open and he stood stock still for a fraction of a second, feet still separated in a stride, arms a-swing at his sides. Wentworth's hand flashed up and forward. He hurled his automatic with all the force of that vertical downward sweep.

The butt of the gun crashed between the man's eyes and his head jerked backward so that the beam of his light struck the ceiling. Wentworth wrenched to free himself from the crevasse, but the belt that held the machine gun ammunition caught on a jagged projection. The man reeled, back to the wall, and a moan wrenched from him. His hands rose toward his face.

Wentworth struggled to get loose. But before he could slip the belt over his head and jerk it free, the man had thrust himself out from the wall and was snatching for the automatic gleaming on the floor.

Wentworth hopped on his one good leg and flung himself bodily on the man, striking with a second gun as they collided heavily. His foot slipped, his blow missed, and he spilled to the ground. The man straightened, leveled the gun. A shot now would be fatal. Wentworth whirled the ammunition drum on the belt and the drum caught the man on the side of the throat just below the ear. He went down like a pole-axed ox.

Wentworth thrust himself up from the floor and shot a swift glance toward the lake. There had been no alarm there. The curves of the tunnel had concealed their battle.

He bent over the man. He was dead, the side of his skull caved in by that last blow. His corpse fitted snugly into the crevasse after his clothes had been stripped from him. Wentworth donned them rapidly, drew the lamp-fitted cap down on his aching temples. But now he was forced to abandon the machine gun. He thrust it into the crack with the dead man, together with the ammunition drum, and armed only with the two automatics, pushed on along the dim passageway.

The man he had killed was about his own build, and as Wentworth moved along, he used materials from his make-up kit, strapped beneath his arm, to alter his complexion to the pasty whiteness of the other's, to sharpen his nose and strap his ears down close to his head. He had had only a glimpse of the other man's walk, but that, too, he imitated, slouching his shoulders and swaying his head slightly from side to side. The limp was inevitable, but he could explain that—

Yes, in the dimly lighted tunnel, he thought he could pass muster.

HE COVERED two twisting miles before lurid lights painting the walls told him he was approaching some other members of the Devil's crew. He bowed his head so that the shadow of his visor was stronger, so that the dazzle of the light would strike into the eyes of any interceptor. He slouched on, rounded the bend of the tunnel carelessly and immediately his keen eyes were at work.

A half dozen men were sprawled out on blankets thrown down on the floor. A dozen oil flares were guttering in niches of the rocks. Four men leaned on elbows to play cards. On a box at the elbow of a fifth card player who sat cross-legged, was a telephone! The man looked up as Wentworth sauntered toward them and stood staring morosely down at the game.

"Want your hand back, Bill?" the man by the telephone asked.

Wentworth said, "Naw. I sprained my ankle on a rock an' I'm sore as hell."

"You're always sore as hell about something," the man sniffed, and looked down at his cards again.

Wentworth stood watching them a while longer, then loafed toward the mouth of the tunnel opposite the one he had entered. There was only that one exit, but Wentworth saw there something that interested him, a line of dump wagons. The stench of the eels was strong about them.

"Where you goin', Bill?" the man by the phone yelled.

"See a man about a dog," Wentworth growled back at him.

The men laughed, and he went on into the darkness that the beam of his cap light rolled back for him. He followed the trail of the wagon wheels around a curve, then began to travel at a shambling run. If he did not return in ten minutes, that bunch back there might get suspicious. He forced himself on.

He wheeled around another curve and checked sharply, staring at a chute that led downward. At its lower end, he could make out the red glare of a fire and that was all. He probed on beyond the chute and found a narrow descending spiral of stairs. On the point of going down, he peered upward and found a ladder of wood led to another such stairway above. As far as his light would carry, the shaft climbed straight upward. The tunnel ended here. From the descending passageway, came the muttering voices of men.

As nearly as Wentworth could estimate it, Jackson had been gone on his way for an hour. It would have taken him three quarters of that time to get to the mouth of the cave. It would be hours before the troops could get here, hours when another great load of the fearful explosive of the Devil could be made and sent out to terrorize the world.

Wentworth tiptoed down the spiral stairs, the light on his cap out, and at the final turn of the steps peered cautiously around it. He saw a vast shadowed chamber whose far wall was lined with great iron vats, before which men stripped to the waist moved ceaselessly back and forth, dipping long, two-handed scoops into them. There were red-glowing fires between them all and from some an evil purplish vapor rose to piped vents above.

The dull, monotonous roar of exhaust fans in the vents sounded through the room. The odor was fetid, rancid with fish oil. This was the laboratory where the Devil's hell-bombs were made!

BARRELS OF chemicals stood about. A man flung a scoopful of white powder from one into a vat and the purple vapor above it turned orange. The man stepped back and dragged a hairy arm across his forehead. Another man, almost horizontal with the effort, was pushing an iron truck along, stacked high with boxes.

Wentworth heard two voices near at hand, pulled back from sight. The words still came to him among the noises of the room, the dull roar of the fan.

"Lousy job," said one. "If it vasn't it pays so vell...."

The other laughed shortly. "A t'ousand a week's big money in any man's town."

"Jawohl!" the other grunted.

"Yeah, but after a few more towns is blowed up, we'll be O.K. Enough of this stuff will be made. We can go out and live like Al Capone."

"But dis rush order that coomes through," the German said doggedly. "That I do not like. It like trouble sounds."

"Sure, you always hunt trouble!"

A telephone bell jangled. "Yeah?" the last speaker answered. "No, ain't seen Bill. What's up?"

Bill! That was what the card player had called Wentworth.

They had taken alarm at his failure to return! If a search party was sent out, he was trapped. There were no side passages from this tunnel, no place to hide….

"Sure, we'll start some men right away," the man was talking again. "Say, what's the rush order about? Hell, we've got enough stuff here to blow half the United States clean off the map. Sure, right away."

Wentworth stole up the stairway and climbed the ladder, labored up the spiral above. Below was sure capture. Undoubtedly the man on the phone would call above, too, but if he could dodge them here in the tunnels for a few hours and keep their attention centered inward while Jackson brought troops….

The steps were steep. Wentworth was already tired. The climb was endless. Doggedly he fought on, his lamp out now so that he might detect the first gleam of an approaching enemy's light. He still had not solved the problem of how the explosive was carried from the cavern laboratory to the woods road where Jackson had seen the truck loaded with it. No boats had appeared on their circuit of the lake, no wheel tracks had marked the far tunnel. There was some other way.

On and on he climbed, and after an hour of that, he stopped sharply, listening. Without warning, a foot rasped over his head!

Wentworth froze in his tracks, waiting to place the footsteps. They were repeated with a hollow sound as if they moved on wood. He realized that they were on flooring close above him. Cautiously he let an instant's light gleam from the cap lamp and saw flooring not twenty feet above him.

He went up the last steps on cat feet. There was a thin gleam of light slatting down from the boarding and Wentworth pressed his eye close to the crack.

He was looking into a naked electric bulb that dangled from a ceiling of crude wooden flooring like the one above him. As he watched, a man's hand reached up and extinguished it and slow steps went up a stairway. An oblong of light fell down upon the man as a trap door above him opened. With a grin that bared his teeth menacingly, Wentworth recognized that lean tall figure. The man above was the Devil!

CHAPTER 20
A DARING PLAN

WHEN THE trapdoor above had been closed, Wentworth pressed upward on his own. It did not yield. Cautiously, he turned on his hat lamp and scanned the lower side of the door. He found a bolt that operated from his side, slid it back and tried again. This time the trapdoor went up soundlessly and with an ease that indicated a counterbalance weight was helping. Gun in hand now, Wentworth stole across the room. He was in the basement of a crude cabin on top the mountain, he found.

If he could eliminate the Devil, destroy those eels from which the explosive was made…. He crept up the second stairway, reached the trapdoor through which the Devil had disappeared, and froze there, listening.

"You damned little wop!" the Devil was saying harshly. "I turn my back and you try to kill Ann."

148

The lazy drawl that answered him was the voice of Angelica Patrici! "You turn your back again, and I'll finish the job," she declared.

The sound of a blow was flat and resounding. A body thudded to the floor above.

Wentworth pressed lightly against the trap door with his finger tips. It did not budge. He pushed harder, got his shoulder against it and heaved—futilely. He heard the snarling sound of Angelica's hate, the mockery of the Devil. Frantically he searched the trap door for some hole to see through, to shoot through. Finally he found a tiny slit and peered upward. Strange to see daylight after all these hours of unrelieved blackness below. Before him was a rough washing stand above which hung a mirror. In that mirror, figures were moving.

A woman, black hair streaming, was wrestling with a man. The man chopped his fist across hard and the woman flew away from him and struck a wall. She stood there, her eyes heavy-lidded with hate, a line of blood at her mouth corner.

"For the last time, my dear Angelica," the man spoke slowly. "Get out and stay out."

Angelica said slowly, "You are going to marry that little blonde witch!"

The Devil's head—Wentworth could see only the back in the mirror—nodded slowly. "She shall be the queen of my empire, of America."

"And that van Sloan woman? She'll be queen of Canada I suppose?" The dark woman was sneering. Her splendid, sullen lips were curled mockingly.

"No," the Devil said. "When I have finished with her, I shall let her head a joint harem for my assistants."

Angelica laughed, and Wentworth felt a rage stir like a hot snake within him. Nita had betrayed him. She was nothing to him any longer. Yet his hand clutched his automatic savagely and strained anew against the trap door that would not yield. He could not fire through these thick boards. Even if he located the exact spot where the Devil stood, the automatic would scarcely be effective. Hell, the man was impervious to ordinary lead anyway. Hadn't the Spider fired a half dozen bullets directly at him and didn't the man still live, hadn't he swum through the lake of eels?

Wentworth drove the wild thoughts from his brain, forced himself to calmness and stared up through the slit again. Angelica was staring at the Devil with wide, frightened eyes, with eyes that would not believe what they saw.

"What have I reserved for you, dear?" the Devil was asking mockingly. "Why, death, my sweet one." He laughed horribly—and the crack of a gun bit through the sound!

AS WENTWORTH stared in the mirror, Angelica seemed to shrink more closely against the wall where she leaned. He could see only her face above the Devil's shoulder. He saw it drain slowly of color, saw the head sag forward and then he saw no more of Angelica, but the Devil twisted aside and a body hit the floor.

Wentworth jerked up his gun, checked a shot with violent effort. Fool that he was, he was about to fire at the mirrored reflection of the Devil! The jangling of the phone calmed his madness. The Devil's feet stumped across the floor, out of the range of the mirror, and his quiet voice came clearly.

"Why bother me with such a small affair? Find Bill and throw him to the eels. Yes, the eels! Yes, the door is bolted." The mechanical clatter of the phone came to Wentworth, but the feet remained stationary. Presently the voice spoke again. "Get the cabin plane ready and put in three boxes of pills. Yes. I'm flying to New York City at once…. Yes, forward the balance through the regular route as soon as possible. I'm not going to launch the attack, just wipe out a few major points and men. The girl goes with me. And, oh yes, you'll find some carrion in my room. Throw it to the eels. We must keep them well fed."

Wentworth waited tensely beneath the planks. Would the Devil pass where he could shoot him? The feet crossed and recrossed the floor above him, then became even heavier, and Wentworth had a momentary glimpse in the mirror of the Devil with Ann Beach's blonde beauty unconscious over his shoulder, stalking toward the door. Then it slammed and Wentworth was alone. Fury gnawed at his brain. The man responsible for all this infamy had been within ten feet of him, yet he had been powerless to act. And the Devil was on his way to murder and loot in New York City itself while Kirkpatrick, summoned to Albany, was miles away from the barricades he should defend.

Well, soon the Devil's men would come to remove the "carrion," which so recently had been a lovely woman, and they would unbolt this door. Then the Spider would begin his vengeance. It was twenty minutes before the door opened above and the feet of two men clumped into the room.

"Criminee!" gulped one. "That guy sure is a devil. He rubbed out the wop."

The man grunted as he bent over the body and lifted. Wentworth crouched beneath the trap door with a gun in each hand. He heard the bolts rasp back. The door was yanked up and he stood erect, covering the two men who carried Angelica's body, one at her head and one at her feet.

"Hold it just like that," Wentworth ordered.

THE MAN in front frowned. "Geez, Bill, what's got into you?"

"That ain't Bill!" the man in back yelped, his eyes grown big with panic.

He was half behind his companion and he went for his gun. The automatic in Wentworth's left hand spoke, and the man spun with his hand on his throat and slapped down on the floor. The corpse of the woman sagged against the back of the second man and he pitched downward toward Wentworth. He jerked himself aside and let the man fall. The man tried to catch himself with his arms and one snapped with a dull crunch as he hit the floor. He moaned and rolled gripping the fractured arm.

"Get up!" Wentworth ordered coldly.

The man moaned again, but under the prod of that leveled gun, he got to his feet and stumbled back up the stairs. At Wentworth's orders he explained the method in which various phones were reached with the instrument there and with a gun in his ear, he repeated into the phone certain orders that Wentworth gave him. All the laboratory workers were to leave the vats and, taking all the guards and everyone else, go to the nets. A call to the guard room back of the nets told them what was happening and stated it was necessary to seine as many eels as possible at once.

When these things had been done, Wentworth picked up an alarm clock, sent the man ahead of him, and stooped to imprint the seal of the Spider on the forehead of the dead man. When his prisoner saw that, he turned white and begged for mercy.

Wentworth stared at him fixedly. "You shall have the same chance for life that I give myself," he said, "if you supply all the information I ask about the caverns."

THE MAN babbled his thanks, and Wentworth's gun urged him once more toward the steps downward. He showed a hidden door on the spiral stairway that opened directly into the magazine and burrowed off through the rock to enter the tunnel to the laboratory by another secret door.

"There's another entrance in the tunnel near the lake," the man said. "It goes all the way around the lake and there's another cave mouth in the side of the mountain. It's built along a fissure Isong found."

"You never built all these tunnels," Wentworth declared.

The man shook his head. "Most of them were here when we dug in from outside. Isong had a map and a flock of papers he never let us see. He said some old monks who dated back God knows how long had found the secret of this explosive while fooling with these eels." The man was frantic in his efforts to

153

please. "He tried to get the park lands first so he could make an extensive search for the cavern. Then he stumbled on it in a prospecting trip and decided not to wait for the bill to pass."

The man eagerly showed Wentworth the entrance to the magazine, a square chamber about twenty feet on a side. His flash light revealed wooden boxes stacked tier on tier, against all the walls and reaching half way to the ceiling. If these boxes were full—Wentworth dragged one down carefully and pulled the slotted top to one side. It was tightly packed with grenades that were heavy with the disintegrator explosive.

Wentworth pocketed six of the grenades, dragged down another box. This was full to the brim with a purplish powder, fine as the dust it would create of mortal beings if any were around when it went off.

"Enough explosive to blow up half the country," the worker had complained in the laboratory.

Wentworth, lips grim, ordered his prisoner across the room where he could watch and spilled the purple powder to the floor, then he placed a grenade in the midst of it and placed a grenade box on top of it. Then he rigged a simple time bomb with the alarm clock. He attached a cord to the alarm clock so that when it rang, the bell clapper would jerk a weight made up of three grenades from a precariously balanced position on the boxes to the floor. He knew the powder was sensitive to concussion from what Jackson had told him of the fright when a truckload of the stuff jarred on the woods road.

The clock registered eleven o'clock. Wentworth set it for noon.

His prisoner stared with desperate eyes.

"In God's name, man," he demanded, "do you know what you're doing?"

Wentworth finished setting the bomb and stood up, staring into his eyes with a reckless, mocking smile on his mouth.

"Surely," he said. "I'm going to blow the whole mountain *up in dust!*"

The man shook his head vehemently, holding out his one good arm in a gesture of appeal. "But don't you realize, it takes a full hour to get out of here. We'll be blown up with it!"

Wentworth's smile turned into flat, mocking laughter. "What are you kicking about?" he demanded. "I promised you the same chance I have. This gives it to you."

CHAPTER 21
BLAST OF JUDGMENT

THE MAN backed away from the madness in Wentworth's eyes, from the fever harshness in his laughter.

"I'll go up the stairs," he said.

Wentworth shook his head slowly. "No," he said.

"We're going to the lake of eels." His gun enforced the statement and the man, back against the stone wall now, shuddered violently.

"Then for God's sake, let's get going!" he cried.

He blundered, staggering through the arched entrance to the magazine. The heavy wooden door slammed shut behind them.

"Have you got a watch?" Wentworth asked casually, and when the man nodded, "Set it for five minutes after eleven."

"Five minutes, five minutes!" The man's teeth chattered with fear. He shambled across the laboratory, his broken arm supported now by a hand tucked into his belt. He passed the smoking vats to huge iron cauldrons where the broth had cooled.

"Wait," said Wentworth. "There is a little necessary precaution to be taken."

He picked up a big iron dipper and scooped up the cold broth in which parts of the eels had been boiled for hours. Deliberately be emptied the contents over his prisoner's clothing, then dumped another scoopful over his shoulders and chest until he too was saturated with the liquid. He was slimy with the stuff and a strong odor of rancid fish oil and musk pervaded the room.

"I don't want that stuff on me," the man protested "In the name of heaven, Spider, let's get away from here. Every minute we wait...."

"Listen, fool," Wentworth swore, "come here or I'll shoot your legs out from under you and leave you to go up in dust. I said I'd give you the same chance I had, and I will if it kills you."

Trembling, fully convinced that he had to deal with a madman, the prisoner crept nearer and Wentworth deluged him with more of the liquid. He doused himself twice more back and front, then limped toward the door, herding the man ahead. The battery was dim in his cap light now and he threw it aside and picked up an oil lantern.

The man raced wildly ahead of Wentworth's dragging pace,

his eyes frantic as he glanced ever and again at the watch strapped to his wrist.

IT WAS half past eleven—thirty minutes before the bomb would explode—when they reached the guard chamber where Wentworth had bluffed his way past the man at the telephone. The man was there, still beside the instrument.

He sprang to his feet.

"Where the hell have you been?" he demanded. "Do you know...." He paused as he made out their oil dripping clothes in the dim light, as he saw the glint of weapons. He cursed and snatched for his pistol on the box by the phone.

Wentworth waited until he got it and drilled him between the eyes. He delayed to print the Spider's seal on his forehead, and the phone bell jangled loudly.

Wentworth, holding his prisoner at a distance, took up the instrument. It would not do for any alarm to be spread yet by a failure to answer.

"Yeah?" he queried.

"Where's Monk?" the voice demanded.

"Seeing a man about a dog."

"Tell him to shoot all the stuff he's got made up here right away," the voice raged. "I can't raise the laboratory and I just got a radio from the chief that there are thousands of troops headed here. I'm working the mines from here, and it will probably take care of most of them, but I want some of the small bombs right away."

Wentworth grinned tightly into the mouthpiece. "Okay, chief," he said.

Wentworth squeezed the trigger, jerking the gun in a sweeping arc across the tunnel.

Wentworth hung up. He saw his prisoner dart into the tunnel way and threw up his gun. But the man was already swallowed in the shadows, his feet slapping heavily on the stone floor.

He would stampede the workers at the lake, drive them into that hidden tunnel he had spoken about, but it would be too late. Only twenty minutes remained now, Wentworth estimated, before the bomb would let go and blow the top of the mountain into dust.

Wentworth had seen what the tiny portion of explosive that a cigar could hold would accomplish. He felt quite confident there was ample to destroy the mountain. He might well die with it himself. But that was a risk he was prepared to take, a risk the Spider always ran. He was traveling at a labored jog now. His strength was all but spent and he must reach the lake if his plan was to succeed. After ten minutes of heavy running he heard commotion, heard feet beat along the tunnel toward him!

The men were not trying to escape, they were coming back for him! Wentworth frowned. That was wrong, of course. They weren't coming for him. They hoped to make the magazine in time to cut off the clock. Perhaps the hidden exit tunnel had jammed and they had no way to cross the lake....

He raced on to meet the men. From the twists of the tunnel, he knew he was within a hundred yards of the spot where he had thrust the dead man and machine gun into a crevasse. If he could reach that—but he must reach it! He must get through these men and reach the lake before the blast ripped out and destroyed every soul in the cavern. He must survive to thwart the Devil who was flying toward New York with enough explosive to blast the entire city off the earth!

He surged around a bend and the darting rays of flashlights fell upon him. A renewed shout burst from the men ahead, a spattering of pistol shots rang like thunder down the tunnel. Chips of stone flew from the walls.

WENTWORTH DID not return the fire. His face was set in a stubborn mold and his burning eyes saw only one thing, the black shadow of the crevasse where the machine gun was hidden. He pounded on at the jog which was the best speed he could make. More lead whined around him. A jerking blow on the top of his head and darkness fell in his path. A bullet had smacked through the light on his cap. Well, that made him safer. He had forgotten it. He drove himself on, chest laboring, his whole body crying out with pain.

More lead sang evilly about him. But the men were not taking time to stop and aim. There was no time to pause if they were to reach the magazine before that bomb let go. Wentworth was doomed anyway, in their minds. Wasn't he running madly upon their guns? Sooner or later, they would drop him.

A bullet plucked at Wentworth's sleeve. He lurched to one side and felt the fan of another. But he was a dark figure against blackness now that his light was out. He forced his failing body on. The men were within fifty feet now, running swiftly. One in front had no gun, but was sprinting like a champion, bound for the magazine to save the others.

Crazily, Wentworth flung a bullet at him—and missed! Wentworth miss! Good lord, he must be near his end, then. He wasted no more lead, but labored on. The crevasse was only twenty feet now, thirty feet from the first of the men.

With a desperate effort, Wentworth threw his last remnant of strength into a final spurt, flung himself face down on the slimy floor and slid the last ten feet. His oily clothes helped him speed on the way and his hands grasped the crevasse while the men were still twenty feet away. One stopped and leveled his pistol. Wentworth rested his automatic on his left forearm and plunked lead into the man's chest. He wilted and Wentworth snatched at the machine gun.

How could those men miss now? A stationary target, brilliantly illuminated by their dozen flashlights, all concentrated upon him. How could they miss? Lead hailed about him. He dragged the machine gun out and frantic panic shouted in that tunnel way. When their aim should have been best, they were terrorized by the menacing snout of a death-spitting weapon. With a sob of thankfulness, Wentworth squeezed the trigger and held the bucking gun down while he jerked its muzzle in a sweeping arc across the tunnel.

"Lights out!" a man shouted. "Down, fla—"

Five slugs cut off his voice, and before the echo of his shout had pierced that hell-blasting gun, the last of his followers had slumped to the earth. Wentworth sprang to his feet and rushed on into the darkness, stooping once to snatch up a flashlight. He laughed with sobbing breath as he ran on. For once the Spider would not mark his prey. What need when that prey would soon be dust!

ON AND on he labored, gripping the machine gun to his

chest with loving arm, the flashlight beam dancing ahead of him like a firefly in the crowding darkness. Scarcely three minutes of that hour's grace could be left now.

In God's name, where was the lake? Even as he uttered that cry in his heart, he saw the beam of the light glisten on the black surface not fifty feet away. Fifty feet? Fifty miles! As he ran, he saw a figure dart out from the wall with one hand raised, the other awkwardly akimbo. His prisoner of the broken arm.

"Save me, Spider!" he cried. "Save me!"

Wentworth's lips bared his teeth in a savage grimace that was meant for mirth. The man's treachery had failed and now he cried to the Spider for mercy.

Wentworth faltered in his stride, plunged against the wall, and nearly fell, leaning there panting. Twenty-five feet to go, twenty-five feet that seemed to stretch into all eternity. The man reached his side.

"How much... time?" Wentworth demanded.

"A minute! Quick Spider, you said the lake!"

Wentworth's words were a hoarse pant of breath, hardly recognizable as human. "Carry me... lake...."

The man braced his one good arm beneath Wentworth's shoulders and together they staggered toward the shelf that thrust out into the lake of eels.

Reeling, they staggered out on the lip of the tunnel.

"Now what?" the man cried. "In God's name, what? Fifteen seconds, fifteen seconds!"

"Dive!" said Wentworth. He stepped to the edge of the water, gulped a deep breath and holding the machine gun in his hands as a diving weight, plunged out into the black lake where the killer eels sported!

As he dived he caught a glimpse of the man with the broken arm staring at him with wide, frightened eyes. The water was ice. It stabbed to the vitals of his superheated body, pierced his wounded thigh with fearful fire. He heard another splash behind him, saw the gleam of red eyes ahead and to every side—and the world fell in upon him!

THERE WAS a terrific upward surge of water that sent him at unbelievable speed toward the surface. Cataclysmic pressure beat down upon him from above. The gun was wrenched from his hands. His arms and legs were like straws in a hurricane, twisted and jerked about as if some malignant force sought to rip them from his body. His mind was stunned. His skull seemed to squeeze in upon his brain. All was darkness and black death about him. Only one thought remained. He must live. The Spider must live. Must... *must... MUST.*

Wentworth's next memory of that holocaust was his ability to breathe. His head was above water and air was rushing into his lungs, and it was light. The hot sun of noontide blazed down upon him through clouds of dust that made the whole sky dull red. But the water was rushing at terrific speed, sucking him at an incredible pace past a shore where stalagmites glistened strangely in the sun. Feebly Wentworth began to work arms and legs. They seemed not to belong to him. There was no feeling there at all.

He drove his limbs by will power, forced them into the familiar rhythm of a crawl, feet lashing at the surface in staccato beat, arms flailing with precise calculation to generate the maximum power. He made no effort to swim against the stream. He went with it and struggled to cut across its force toward that whirling shore that was only ten feet away. Ten feet—but he was on the verge of absolute exhaustion. The cold of the water had braced him for the moment, but his body was tired, tired. The excitement and the need had nerved him to the use of his feeble left leg, but that, too, was faltering beneath the new and terrific demands Wentworth made upon it.

He felt that his stroke was weak, that he was the plaything of the waters, but slowly he gained on that rush of titan force, slowly, slowly, until, thrusting a leg downward, he felt the swift cutting drag of the shore beneath his feet.

Wentworth never knew how he dragged himself from the water, how he drove himself to his wobbling legs, but he knew that presently he found himself staring down into the deep valley of what had been an underground lake, steaming now as it dried beneath the first sunlight that ever had penetrated those subterranean depths, spotted with the carcasses of slimy snake-like things that were the killer eels of the red eyes.

In the valley's bottom was a rent and into that the last of the waters had gurgled. Wentworth stared down upon it and began to cackle with mad mirth. The mountain had disappeared! It had been wiped off the face of the earth as though it had never been, atomized, disintegrated by the terrific concussion of that explosion! With it had gone the Devil's crew, the cauldrons of hell-brew that were to become this explosive. The very means of its creation was gone now that the eels had been destroyed.

Yet somewhere above soared the Devil with his destroying thunderbolts, with Ann Beach still captive, the Devil ready to ravage New York to add other millions to those he had pillaged.

The Spider stared up into the dusty red vault of the sky, into the burning sun that was like a glowering eye. He shook his fist at the heavens, and stood and screamed with laughter.

"They've paid now," he cried, "they've paid. It's the Blast of Judgment!"

He pitched forward on his face, conquered at last by unconsciousness.

CHAPTER 22
CRAZY MAN

"**T**HE MAN is crazy!"

Wentworth heard those words and a protest started in his throat. He held it back and pushed his head up through the black water that was trying to strangle him. He kept his eyes closed.

"The man is crazy, I tell you," the voice repeated harshly. "He's been babbling about man-killing eels and caverns and the Devil or something."

"He'll be all right, sir," another man insisted. "If you'll just let me... Mr. Kirkpatrick! Thank God, you've come, sir. They're trying to ship the major off to...."

"Quite right, Jackson." The familiar clipped tones were those of Stanley Kirkpatrick.

Wentworth forced his eyelids apart, and pain stabbed through them. He squinted but kept them open and once more words came to his throat, a faint croak. "Stanley, Stanley!" He shook his head violently, trying to clear his eyes, to drive the blackness from his brain. "Kirk! We must hurry!"

He felt a cool, firm hand on his head. "It's all right, Dick, old man."

"All right, hell!" Wentworth's voice broke out violently, hoarse but recognizable now. "The Devil is flying on New York, Kirk, with bombs, Kirk." He thrust his weary body upward.

"I'll take care of that," Kirkpatrick assured him. "It's just a matter of shooting him down if he doesn't surrender."

"Bombs are in the plane! Its fall would wreck twenty square miles!" He struggled against the hands holding him and lashed out savagely with his fist. Things were clearing now. He saw two white-coated men, saw the blaze of sunlight and recognized that he was still in a field near the mountain.

"Strychnine, Doctor," he ordered harshly. "Do I have to tell you your business?"

The doctor's white-coated shoulders shrugged.

"Mad, I tell you!" His angular face was stubborn.

"Strychnine!" Wentworth said violently. "And give me a flask of brandy."

He got what he wanted, that gaunt worn man sitting erect on the stretcher, his clothing torn, his body racked with pain and fatigue, but eyes still burning with command. Immediately the clouds of blackness drove entirely from his brain. He gurgled brandy and its warmth sent needles of new life pricking over his body. He thrust himself to his feet. He wavered, but waved help aside.

"There's no time to be lost, Kirk. Get me to a plane." His voice was brisk and decisive, despite the glassiness in his eyes.

Kirkpatrick stood before the swaying man who was his friend. "Look here, Dick," he said. "The doctor says that wound in your leg is a week old, that crease on your skull is days old, too. You've been working when you ought to be in the hospital."

"And because I did," Wentworth snapped, "the Devil can't make any more of that infernal explosive of his!"

Kirkpatrick took a short step forward, grasped Wentworth's shoulders with both hands. "Do you mean it, Dick?"

Wentworth cursed. "What do you think I am, a radio comedian?"

Kirkpatrick's eyes gleamed. His lips smiled grimly.

"O.K. You're the boss. What do you want?"

"A fast plane. A doctor to go on the plane with me and you. Jackson, get me a saber from the troops, one with an edge that will cut. Phone a warning to New York."

His orders came like bullets. He peered with his harsh glare at the angular, tall doctor who had called him crazy.

"You're going with me," he said flatly. "Get the stuff to make a cast for this damned leg and take it with us."

"Go to hell," said the doctor, his bony face flushed, his sharp jaw set.

"I've been there," Wentworth said grimly. His hand went to his belt. His gun wasn't there. He shook his head sharply. "Kirk, make the fool see sense."

IN THE end, he got what he wanted. Half an hour later, the cabin plane took off, tearing the air toward New York. The lanky doctor, still red-faced with anger, was working over a cast for his leg.

"You're going to lose that leg surer than hell," he said as he mixed plaster in a bowl. "It's ripe for gangrene right now and this cast will help that along splendidly. That leg should be excised and then strapped up and drained for three weeks."

"Tonight," said Wentworth grimly, "you can do what you damned please to that leg, but right now, make that cast so the leg can't bend. I've got to walk on it presently, and walk damned spryly."

"I'll probably amputate tonight." The doctor's sharp jaw snapped on the words.

Wentworth leaned back and closed his eyes. He was tired. "What happened at Albany?" he asked dully. "How did Jackson get you to the mountain so soon?"

"Jackson?" asked Kirkpatrick. "Nita sent us there. At least she sent us out the Ausable Chasm road, and your explosion did the rest. Incidentally in ten minutes more, the soldiers would have been over the most complete system of mines I've ever heard of. Your explosion set them off."

Jackson broke in. "Begging the major's pardon sir, but I learned over the phone that troops already were on the way and I came back."

"Jackson found you and carried you two miles to the ambulance," Kirkpatrick said.

"It was only a little over a mile," Jackson muttered. "What I can't see, sir, is how you lived in that water with the eels long enough to get out again."

Wentworth smiled with his eyes closed. "I put oil from the eels all over my clothing. The eels never attack their own kind and I suppose the oil turned me into a big eel to them."

"Lord, sir, you had time to think of that, when…"

Wentworth jerked his head impatiently. "Kirk, you said Nita sent you. That means Albany was saved?"

"More or less," Kirkpatrick agreed. "Nita—"

He hesitated, but got no encouragement from Wentworth. "Nita said she thought you were out of your head. After seeing that wound, I can believe it."

Wentworth said grimly, "I wasn't out of my head when I saw Nita." He lifted his head and stared at the air speed indicator on the forward wall of the plane. "Kirk, what's the situation in New York? What guards and so on?"

Kirkpatrick told him, in detail.

"But they won't do any good," Wentworth said wearily. "Only one thing can do any good and that's the death of the Devil. And bullets won't touch him. I know now how he saved himself from the eels, but bullets—it's not a steel vest." His hand touched the cavalry sword at his side. Jackson had whetted it to a razor edge.

"Can't we get some word on the radio about whether anything has happened in New York?" Wentworth asked. "I'm afraid we'll be too late."

"That fellow Pierce ought to be on about now," Kirkpatrick said, throwing the switch on the radio and setting the dial.

"Then you didn't arrest him?" Wentworth's query was quick.

"I couldn't find him when you called and Finnegan wired me he didn't think we could make a charge stick against him." Kirkpatrick's eyes were keen on Wentworth's face as he spoke. The radio began to crackle as the tubes warmed, and a faint dynamic voice began to pound out words. They were unintelligible at first, but gradually the staccato delivery of Pierce became understandable.

"**THIS MAN** who signs himself the Devil has given the mayor until six o'clock tonight to deliver seventy-five million into his hands on pain of throwing the switch on the radio and blowing up half the city. There is no doubt of his ability to wipe most of New York off the map. The explosive he uses absolutely disintegrates everything within range. Why, a few days ago, he murdered Senator Beach with a cigar.

"That small bit of explosive in his cigar was cataclysmically effective. It knocked down the columns in the capitol building a full city block away. It killed a half dozen men and women in the park. It wrecked automobiles in the streets...."

"Don't you see?" Wentworth demanded. "The man is spreading terror like a man sowing wheat. Five minutes after he finishes that talk, the mobs will be howling at the city hall for immediate surrender of that seventy-five millions."

He broke off to listen to Pierce's voice.

"It is five-forty-five now. In fifteen minutes, the mayor of New York must pay seventy-five millions into the hands of one of the most ruthless criminals this world has ever known—or be prepared to have his city swept by blasts more powerful than the big brother of T.NT. which is called trinitrotoluene. After all, other explosives merely have impact. This one tears the very atoms apart!"

Pierce signed off and another news announcer took up the story.

"Stand by a minute. Here you are, a flash right from the mayor's office. The mayor has decided to pay!"

Kirkpatrick and Wentworth were staring fixedly into each other's eyes. "There isn't anything else he can do," the police commissioner muttered.

"No," said Wentworth. "Were you able to get anything on Peter Isong?"

Kirkpatrick shook his head. "So far as I can discover, there isn't any such man. No trace of him has been found in any records in the country or in immigration offices."

Wentworth nodded slowly. "I expected that. Do you know the plans for collecting the ransom?"

KIRKPATRICK STRODE forward to the pilot's cockpit and spoke hurriedly with the flier at the controls. Two minutes later he was striding back.

"I got Finnegan by radio. He says the Devil will call in person for the money, but at the first sign of treachery one of his men will close a switch that will blow up the city. He says that he will have a dozen men watching him with glasses from various points."

"Where will the delivery be?"

"On the steps of City Hall."

Wentworth glanced at a clock. "Ten minutes to go."

"We're landing now at New York."

"Stop the pilot, tell him to head over the city."

Kirkpatrick stared at Wentworth. "You have a plan?"

"A dozen," snapped Wentworth. "Hurry." When the order had been given, he explained. "When the Devil drives away from the city hall, trail his car from above. You will have over an hour of daylight. As soon as he is clear of the city, and alone upon the road, bomb him out of existence."

"But the bombs! We haven't any."

Wentworth smiled and thrust his hands into his pockets and began pulling out the small baseball-like bombs of the Devil. "This is his own medicine," he said. He thrust himself up on the cast that bound his leg and tested it. He winced once, but nodded his head in satisfaction.

"That's fine," he said. "Good work, Doc, and remember, get the hospital ready for me tonight."

The doctor said, "Nuts."

Kirkpatrick was watching him with tight eyes. "What the hell are you going to do?"

Wentworth reached into a rack on the wall and drew down a parachute pack.

"I'm going to the Devil, I hope," he grinned. "If he escapes you, I hope to be able to locate him. You're not forgetting that Ann Beach is in his power still?"

"No," said Kirkpatrick. "I'm not forgetting. She's going to be in the automobile with him."

Wentworth, buckling on the straps of the parachute, turned to look at him with heavy-lidded eyes. "Quite," he said. His

173

own face was white now with a pain that did not come from his leg. He walked heavily to the door, gesturing to Jackson. "Get the pilot to go over Central Park, Kirk, will you please?"

Jackson put his shoulder to the door and pressed it open against the thrust of slip-stream and the wind of their nearly two-hundred mile speed. The plane streaked northward over Manhattan. Wentworth peered down. The towers of the elaborate hotels just south of the park were directly under him. He saw the vortex crown of the Park Lane….

He stepped off into space.

CHAPTER 23
THE RED CLOAK

HURTLING DOWNWARD toward the greenery of Central Park, Wentworth delayed yanking the rip cord so as to attract as little attention as possible.

When he was barely five hundred feet from the earth, he yanked the cord. He threw his sword ahead of him just before he reached the earth and spilled heavily in the middle of a roadway. Brakes screamed as autos jerked to a halt to avoid running him down.

Wentworth sprang to his feet and hurriedly unstrapped the harness. A cab rolled up beside him and the man leaned out.

"Taxi, mister!" he grinned impudently.

Wentworth nodded, threw the harness after the parachute to the roadside, and vaulted to the car, sword in hand. His leg had been easy a few moments before, but now it had a thousand devils of pain.

"Wireless tower!" he ordered. The cab sped toward the broadcasting headquarters of the International system. When they were a half block from it, Wentworth leaned forward and called, "Park here." He sat back and waited.

Within five minutes, he saw a man cross the pavement and enter a waiting car.

"Follow that!" said Wentworth, and money persuaded the driver. It was neither a long nor tedious pursuit. The man descended from the car ahead in front of the elaborate apartment, Riverside Tower. Great heavens, this was where Nita lived! For a moment after Kirkpatrick had reported her assistance in finding the cavern, Wentworth had felt hope leap within him, but that was destroyed now. If this man was entering Nita's apartment....

Wentworth paid off the cab and went in the house's trade entrance. A man in blue dungarees got in his way. Wentworth knocked him out, tied him up, and ran the service elevator upward to Nita's floor.

He picked the lock of the door and eased in, the heavy cavalry sword bare in his hand. He was in a large foyer that Nita's tasteful hands had decorated, and through a columned arch, he could make out the end of a davenport. Wentworth moved stealthily to the column beside the entrance and stood tensely, listening.

A mocking voice was talking. It was deep and resonant and Wentworth recognized again what he had ascertained when last he had heard J. Osborne Pierce broadcast. It was a quality in the radio commentator's voice that was identical with that of the Devil! That fact and the man's readiness to spread terror through his talks had led Wentworth to trail him. And the way had led to Nita's apartment!

It was easily possible for Pierce to have done all the things the Devil had done. Pierce's presence in Albany coincided with the Devil's appearances there. And when the Devil came to New York, Pierce was here, too. Not much to hang a case on a man, a similarity of voice, a coincidence of being in the same place at identical times. But he knew definitely that Angelica Patrici knew Pierce well, and Angelica had been slain by the Devil because, apparently, she was jealous of Ann Beach. Yes, it all fitted in, now that the trick of speech, that certain intonation of voice had coupled the two men. He grasped the razor-keen blade and started forward. But, hearing Nita's name mentioned, he paused again.

"... She is riding in your place, Ann dear," the mocking voice said.

"Don't call me dear!" The clear voice of Ann Beach quivered with suppressed fury. Wentworth's eyes narrowed. Ann Beach had been supposed to ride in the car that collected the ransom, her life an additional hostage against attack on the Devil. It was Nita who was riding in her place. Then Nita was in the car that Kirkpatrick was to bomb into dust!

TRAITOR THOUGH Wentworth felt Nita was, the thought of her fair beauty destroyed by that devastating blast, made him tremble.

"Very well, Ann darling." The mocking voice was mirthful. "But you may as well get used to it. You're mine, you know, my reward for faithful service! Isong decided on Nita in the end."

The man's slurring laughter made Wentworth's teeth clench, his hand tighten upon his sword. But the girl made no answer. Presently the man went on. "Nita, the dear child, thinks she still has us fooled very neatly."

Wentworth frowned. Isong had taken Nita! But he had figured Pierce and Isong were the same man! Hell, had he slipped up here at the last moment? Had he left Kirkpatrick to take the leader while he bothered with minions of the gang? He forced himself to wait while he listened....

"I'll admit Nita had us fooled for a while. She discovered we had a dictograph and an automatic movie camera hidden in Howard's apartment, and when Wentworth walked in she called the police and fired a shot at him. That convinced us that Howard had succeeded in buying her over of course, when we had heard the dictograph record and seen the film.

He laughed heartily and in the half-darkness of the hall Wentworth cursed himself. Nita had fooled them, the man said. Good God. When he had thought her treacherous, she had been playing shrewdly to wrest their secrets from them, the secrets that later had carried the troops to the cavern! And he, he had accused Nita of treachery.

She had trusted his acute mind to fathom her trick, and he had failed her. It had been madness, the madness of his pain, of his fevered brain. And this man of the mocking voice, this fiend… Dear God! Kirkpatrick was flying to blow up that motorcar with Nita and Isong and the city's wealth!

He must destroy this man, race to rescue Nita and yet keep Isong from blowing up the city. He must force this man to tell how to do that in time, to-

Wentworth's lips twisted away from his teeth in a grin of fury. His eyes turned to flame. But even with his sword raised, he paused, listening.

The man was bragging. "Isong only thinks he's going to get away, though. He's going to blow up the city as soon as he takes off in his plane from Armonk. Wants to wipe out pursuit, give the city so much to think about that he'll get clean away. But he won't, he won't!" He laughed, mocking as the Devil. "I've rigged time bombs in the plane. I've got it all figured out in seconds. He'll blow up the city as soon as he gets a thousand feet of altitude. Within seconds after he does that, the time bombs will let go. And Isong *will go up in dust!*"

Good God in heaven! This fiendish gang was going to destroy the city even though the ransom had been paid! This man had time bombs in the plane, true. But they would not explode until Isong had destroyed the city. And when they did let go, Nita would die. He must hurry, hurry!

His sword a gleam of steely flame, Wentworth sprang into the room.

THE FIGURES of a man and woman were outlined against the purple light of a wide studio window that covered the whole width of the room. As Wentworth sprang into view, the man whirled and his right hand jerked up. The gun splashed crimson fire into the room, and lead whizzed past Wentworth's face. Before the man could fire again, Ann had sprung toward him and seized his gun hand.

The man struggled vainly to wrest the gun from Ann and jerked free as Wentworth thrust with the heavy sword. He stumbled backward, leaving the weapon in the girl's hand, sprang toward a grand piano that filled one side of the room. Ann threw up the gun and fired, but just a second too late. Pierce had yanked a crimson scarf from the piano and flung it before himself.

Suddenly Wentworth understood why his bullets had failed to kill. That scarf must be made of the bullet-proof silk the British had used during the war!* It was thick and heavy and

---

* AUTHOR'S NOTE: The bullet proof qualities of silk are not generally known, but during the World War, the government made extensive experiments with all forms of modern armor and silk came in for its part. The British Government actually equipped four hundred men in each division with a thick silken necklet. It was abandoned later because of its great cost—$25 each. I quote below some excerpts from *Helmets and Body Armor in Modern Warfare,* by Bashford Dean, who was in charge of United States experimentation. Major (or Doctor—he is entitled to both prefixes) Dean went back into history for the first use of silk and cited that the Japanese used padded silk for armor, from the seventh century up until 1870. They often reinforced it with steel plates. He finds it also was used until quite recently in Russia and Germany. Major Dean quotes from William A. Taylor, a British army experimentist: (Helmets and body etc., page 288 footnote.) "The only material that gives materially better results

though the bullet jerked at it, the man behind charged straight toward them now and Wentworth saw a glint of steel. He grasped a rapier in his right hand!

"I'll take him, Ann!" Wentworth cried.

He threw himself on guard, sword held warily as a foil across his palm. It was heavy, and its weight dragged at his enfeebled strength. The man lunged at him viciously with a straight-arm thrust, and Wentworth easily turned it past his shoulder, thrust in riposte and was parried neatly. That one touch of wrist pressure told Wentworth that he had a formidable opponent.

than manganese steel is pure woven silk which, against shrapnel bullets up to a velocity of 900–1,000 foot seconds, has a distinct advantage, weight for weight, over steel." Major Dean also quotes Captain Ley of the Munitions Board, in London. "Bombs were exploded in the fragmentation but at Wembley. Sample pads of silks were used for comparison with plates of helmet steel of twice their weight; the silk pads were the better."

As compared with the specified resistance against bullets of 900 to 1,000 foot seconds, let me quote from the same book; page 298. A forty-five calibre Army automatic, admittedly one of the hardest shooting American, arms, has a foot second velocity of only 802 when the muzzle is against the target! That figure is less, of course, at increasing distances. Let no one suppose, however, that the silk meant here is the kind a woman uses in her dress. Usually raw silk, between layers of weather resistant cloth, was used and that mentioned by Mr. Taylor had a weight of almost eleven ounces to the square foot. Despite its notable success in tests, it was not extensively used because it was expensive and deteriorated so quickly when exposed to the rain and mud of the trenches.

Yet he must triumph at once, or Nita… Wentworth reeled back from a savage attack. The sword zipped past, and Ann cried out, her arm pierced. There was a crash of glass.

"Dick! Dick!" she gasped. "The gun went out the window!"

The man was attacking again, the dim light at his back. Even in the darkness, Wentworth could make out the gleam of his teeth, the glitter of his eyes. He laughed mockingly. "You first, Wentworth, then your lady friend. That hole in her arm will keep Ann busy for a while!"

The words infuriated Wentworth, but the heat was burned out of his brain. His anger was cold now as arctic night, and as black. He thrust and Pierce threw himself sideways to escape, dodged a side slash with the blade. Wentworth slid forward in a furious thrust, missed and drew his left foot up behind him of necessity, since he could not recover on the cast leg. He narrowly missed the point of the rapier at his throat, slapped it aside with his palm, saw his chance as the man retreated and swung the broad sword in a vicious cut.

The blow missed Pierce, but smacked the rapier from his hand. Pierce made no effort to recover. He charged close against Wentworth where he could not be stabbed with the blade and struck savagely with his fist. Wentworth could not dodge. He rolled the blow, but reeled with the impact, staggering back. Pierce came on, hitting hard. Wentworth dropped the sword with a gallantry his foe would not have shown, and closed with him.

But he was seriously handicapped. His leg was a hindrance rather than a help and Pierce, aware of the disadvantage, rushed him continually. Wentworth felt his strength panting out through his laboring lungs. He stood up to the attack, threw himself forward and blocked the hammering blows with his elbows. He reached up and seized Pierce by the throat.

Blows rained upon his body, hammering the breath from him. A kick against his injured leg knocked it out from under him and the two men pitched to the floor. But Wentworth still clung with hands like steel.

Pierce's blows became more feeble. Wentworth was the master now and he must force this man to talk. Ann was half across the room, leaning weakly against the window, clasping her pierced arm. If she released her wrist, she would bleed to death.

Wentworth eased the pressure on Pierce's throat, let a thin stream of air trickle through into his throat.

"Talk and you shall live," he whispered grimly. "Refuse and you die." His whisper grew mocking. "The Spider speaking!" **PIERCE TRIED** to roll his head, raised a hand feebly and Wentworth eased the pressure still more.

"What do you want to know," gasped Pierce hoarsely.

"Where are the bombs?" Wentworth demanded. "Where are the switches that control them?"

Pierce tossed his arms about on the floor. "Only one switch. In plane Isong's using."

"The Devil!"

"Yes, he's the Devil," Pierce agreed. "No more switches except in car and in plane." His voice was easier now. "Just a trick on the city, all those men the Devil said would be watching him."

Wentworth cursed, staring down at the face beneath him,

and suddenly he realized that the man he held was not Pierce! He looked much like him. He had that same mocking timber of voice, but bits of disguise had come off in the struggle and Wentworth saw now that this man was merely a dummy for J. Osborne Pierce. Then, the real Devil was in the car with Nita, was fleeing with the city's millions, was planning to destroy the city by the simple act of closing a small switch in the plane….

Wentworth gasped out a sudden curse, lurching to the right. He saw suddenly why this false Pierce had talked. In those few seconds of revelation, he had tossed his arm about until he could reach the rapier and now, grasping it near the point, he was thrusting savagely at Wentworth's throat!

Wentworth could not ward that blow without taking a hand from the man's throat. If he did that, his weakened hold could be broken and this man might well overpower a pain-wracked Spider. Grimly Wentworth deliberately took the blade in his left shoulder. He clung desperately with both clenching hands to the man's throat—and then he did an heroic thing.

He deliberately twisted his shoulder against the steel, feeling it tear the muscles. But his flesh imprisoned the blade. His foe could not withdraw it to strike again!

For moments they clung like that, both weakening, Wentworth's blood dripping upon the man he strangled. Then the false Pierce went limp. Wentworth squeezed harder, putting the weight of his body upon his rigid arms, held it for long moments, then thrust himself up to his feet. He jerked the rapier free, staggered as the inrushing air brought fierce cutting pain to his wound. He fought off the blackness of unconsciousness, reeled to Ann's side and, one-handed, knotted a handker-chief about her arm which could be twisted into a tourniquet to stop the blood.

Wentworth stumbled away from her then.

"Wait," cried Ann. "Let me bind your shoulder."

Wentworth seemed not to hear. He reached the phone, called police to radio a message to Kirkpatrick.

"The only switch to the bombs is in the Devil's car and in the plane. Destroy both!" he sent word.

WHILE HE talked, Ann had found linen in the bath and, one-handed, bound a crude bandage over his new wound. She heard only his last words, and a cry gasped in her throat.

"But Nita is in the car!" she said hoarsely.

Wentworth turned to her and his face was aged with lines of grief and care. "I know it," he said quietly. "It is her life against the lives of thousands in the city!"

He caught up his sword and the Devil's red cloak in his right hand and the two stared at each other. Wentworth dragged the forearm of his sword hand across his forehead heavily, stood sagging an instant, then limped toward the door.

"Come," he ordered.

They went together to the elevator. The operator stared, bug-eyed, at the two of them, bloodstained and fainting.

"Get this lady to a hospital at once," Wentworth ordered curtly. Even words were a terrific effort. Ann protested, but he shook his head and took a taxi alone.

"Get to Armonk airport," he ordered the driver. "Bronx Parkway! And fast, fast!"

184

It was dark when they reached Kensico dam, still more than five miles from Armonk airport. The cut of the air had partly restored Wentworth and, as the cab raced up the sharp grade around the dam, whirled on along the shore of the Kensico reservoir, he made out the red and green lights of a plane in the air. Could that be the Devil already aloft? Or was it Kirkpatrick closing in for the kill!

"Hurry!" he cried hoarsely.

The cab squealed into a right angle curve, raced, with its rear still swinging, along the Armonk road. Ahead, Wentworth heard a terrific blast!

Good God in heaven! Was he already too late? Had Kirkpatrick bombed the car, killed Nita? The driver skidded to a halt and Wentworth, a half-sob in his throat, slid the heavy two-edged steel of his sword through the window at him. The man stepped on the gas.

The car spun around a curve and the white fence of the airport, blown flat, showed on their right. Ahead their lights threw black shadows into a crater that cut across the road. Far out on the field, a plane was lashing the air with its propeller, illuminated as a circular blur by the floodlights. The Devil and Nita had left the car in time then, and reached their aircraft! Nita was safe for the moment, but already Kirkpatrick's plane was slanting down for the new attack.

If Kirkpatrick even opened fire on that plane, he would set off the bombs! Everything, every human being within hundreds of yards would perish—and that meant Nita and Kirkpatrick and the Spider....

"Over that fence!" Wentworth yelled hoarsely. "Head for that plane that's taking off."

THE LEVELED sword enforced his command and the cab lurched over the ditch, over the fence and charged across the field toward the plane that was slowly gathering speed. It was apparent, even as the cab roared forward, that they would arrive too late.

"Halt!" Wentworth shouted and the man slammed on his brakes instantly.

Wentworth lurched to his knees on the floor, scrambled out to the ground with the Devil's cloak and sword still in his hand. The ship was roaring straight toward him. Its tail was already clear of the ground and in a second it would lift and soar. It would clear the cab, all right, by a few feet.

Wentworth staggered away from the cab. He began to swing the cavalry sword in vertical circles as the taxi spurted away. One, two, three times, he whirled the blade and each circuit nearly jerked him off his feet, so weak was he. The plane was almost upon him now. Wentworth loosed the sword and flung it in a glittering arc directly into the path of the plane! The effort spilled him flat on the ground. He rolled, staring upward.

The sword glinted in the floodlights of the field for an instant, then there was a tremendous, crashing burst of sound as sword and propeller met. The ship shivered in its flight. The blade had smashed the propeller.

Now let the Devil explode the bombs in the city! His radio depended upon the motor, and the pilot must cut the motor at once, or crash his ship.

Wentworth struggled to his feet. He saw that Kirkpatrick's plane, instead of circling to the attack, had slanted to a landing. Even as he watched, it set three points down on earth.

But Wentworth's eyes were all for the Devil's ship. The motor had cut instantly, the nose had bitten into a dive, but the plane was wobbling frightfully.

If the pilot could bring it down without too much jarring, Nita would be saved. If he smashed up, the bombs would let go. Wentworth hurried to be close to the landing. If the bombs let go, he wanted to go too. His work was done, now....

The wobble of the plane lessened. The prompt cutting of the motor had eased the terrific vibration of the smashed propeller. It slanted down, hit awkwardly on its front wheels, bounced once and came down swiftly again. Wentworth could see by the wrenching of the ailerons, the kicking of the rudder how the pilot fought for control. He limped on. The ship set its tail down, almost touched a wing at the same time, then righted itself.

Wentworth raced on frantically. He megaphoned his right hand. "That plane is going to blow up! Bombs aboard!"

He cried that over and over as he drew nearer to the now stationary ship. He kept directly behind its tail where bullets from the windows could not hit him.

"That plane has got a time bomb in it," he shouted. "That plane...."

The door of the ship flung open and a man in helmet and goggles jumped out. He had a suitcase in his hand. "You damned fool!" he shouted. "You smashed my propeller."

187

Wentworth ran on toward him. The pilot came toward him angrily, and suddenly he jerked up a revolver. Wentworth flaunted the Devil's cloak before himself like a shield. The cloak jerked with the bullet's impact, but protected Wentworth. He snapped a single quick shot, and the man pitched forward with collapsing knees. The Spider raced on to the plane, found a man unconscious on the floor, Nita struggling with bonds. He cut the binding ropes, panting out words.

"Time bomb in plane. Get away fast."

He sliced the last rope and Nita staggered to her feet.

"Run," he said. "Run!" He struggled to lift the unconscious man from the floor, the real pilot the Devil had knocked out. Eager hands helped him, the men from Kirkpatrick's plane.

"Run!" Wentworth screamed. "This plane is loaded with time bombs!"

OTHER HANDS picked up the man he tried to lift, picked Wentworth up also and he felt himself borne swiftly away. He fought until he saw that Nita was safe, that the suitcase he was sure carried the ransom was safe. Then he sagged forward, a mad laughter in his brain. The Devil's cloak had saved them all in the end. He did not hear the ripping blast that blew the plane into fragments too small to see, that slapped him and the men who carried him flat, but did not otherwise injure any of them.

Somewhere, later, in a dream he thought that he clung to Nita's hands and cried, "Nita! Nita! In heaven's name, forgive me! You were right. You saved us all from the Devil. And I suspected you. Darling, please…."

In the dream, it seemed to him that Nita's white hand stopped the rush of his words, that Nita's hand caressed his head and that the smile on her lips was ineffably tender.

"Poor boy," this vision in the dream murmured. "There was never anything to forgive. It looked bad for me, and the fever of your wound was in your brain…."

It must have been a long time afterward that Wentworth looked up from his tumbled pillow into the doctor's sharp, always angry face. He looked from that to his bandaged left leg that slung to a brace above his bed. Tubes led from the leg to bottles. He stared down at his right arm, strapped close against his chest.

He rolled his head slowly and saw Nita in a chair beside the bed and suddenly Wentworth knew that the dream of her forgiveness was no vision but reality. He looked at her and grinned and reached out his free hand to hers. Then he glowered up at the doctor.

"You're a lousy sawbones," he grunted. "Couldn't even amputate while I was unconscious. I was too good for you."

The doctor's angular head shook jerkily. "I have never in my life seen a wound so abused and yet have gangrene fail to develop. You are a most remarkable specimen."

Nita said hesitantly, "Then he won't lose his leg?"

"Of course not," grunted Dr. Nurz. He continued to frown down at Wentworth, and touched his leg so that pain shot through it. He grumbled, "How do you feel?"

Wentworth scowled up at him. "Like the Devil," he said, then grinned. "Well, maybe not quite like the Devil we both have in mind."

POPULAR PUBLICATIONS
HERO PULPS

LOOK FOR MORE SOON!

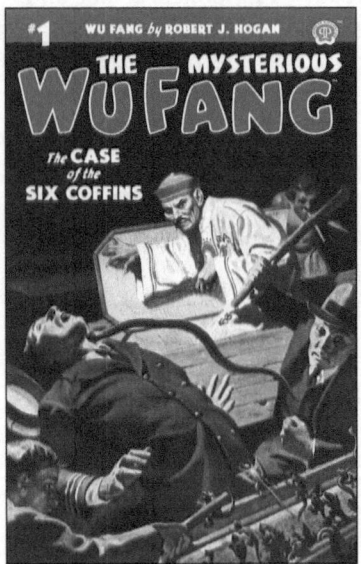

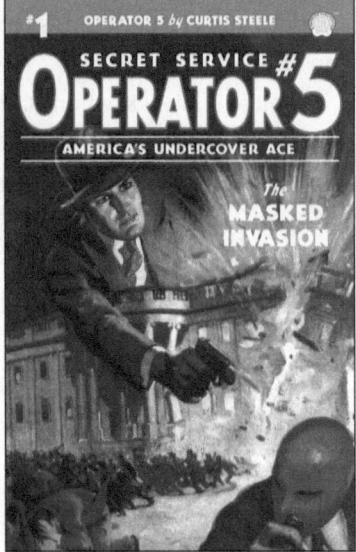

POPULAR HERO PULPS AVAILABLE NOW:

THE SPIDER
- #1: The Spider Strikes — $13.95
- #2: The Wheel of Death — $13.95
- #3: Wings of the Black Death — $13.95
- #4: City of Flaming Shadows — $13.95
- #5: Empire of Doom! — $13.95
- #6: Citadel of Hell — $13.95
- #7: The Serpent of Destruction — $13.95
- #8: The Mad Horde — $13.95
- *NEW:* #9: Satan's Death Blast — $13.95

OPERATOR 5
- #1: The Masked Invasion — $13.95
- #2: The Invisible Empire — $13.95
- #3: The Yellow Scourge — $13.95
- #4: The Melting Death — $13.95
- *NEW:* #5: Cavern of the Damned — $13.95

CAPTAIN SATAN
- #1: The Mask of the Damned — $13.95

THE MYSTERIOUS WU FANG
- #1: The Case of the Six Coffins — $12.95
- #2: The Case of the Scarlet Feather — $12.95
- #3: The Case of the Yellow Mask — $12.95
- #4: The Case of the Suicide Tomb — $12.95
- #5: The Case of the Green Death — $12.95
- #6: The Case of the Black Lotus — $12.95
- #7: The Case of the Hidden Scourge — $12.95

G-8 AND HIS BATTLE ACES
- #1: The Bat Staffel — $13.95

DUSTY AYRES AND HIS BATTLE BIRDS
- #1: Black Lightning! — $13.95
- #2: Crimson Doom — $13.95
- #3: The Purple Tornado — $13.95
- #4: The Screaming Eye — $13.95
- #5: The Green Thunderbolt — $13.95
- #6: The Red Destroyer — $13.95
- #7: The White Death — $13.95
- #8: The Black Avenger — $13.95
- #9: The Silver Typhoon — $13.95
- #10: The Troposphere F-S — $13.95
- #11: The Blue Cyclone — $13.95
- #12: The Tesla Raiders — $13.95

DR. YEN SIN
- #1: Mystery of the Dragon's Shadow — $12.95
- #2: Mystery of the Golden Skull — $12.95
- #3: Mystery of the Singing Mummies — $12.95

MAVERICKS
- #1: Five Against the Law — $12.95
- #2: Mesquite Manhunters — $12.95
- #3: Bait for the Lobo Pack — $12.95
- #4: Doc Grimson's Outlaw Posse — $12.95
- #5: Charlie Parr's Gunsmoke Cure — $12.95